Between Two Skies

Joanne O'Sullivan

CANDLEWICK PRESS

First edition 2017

Library of Congress Catalog Card Number pending
ISBN 978-0-7636-9034-2

17 18 19 20 21 22 BVG 10 9 8 7 6 5 4 3 2 1

Printed in Berryville, VA, U.S.A.

This book was typeset in Granjon.

Candlewick Press
99 Dover Street
Somerville, Massachusetts 02144

visit us at www.candlewick.com

33614080505398

To Andrew, Maeve, and Finn,
my home no matter where we are

Now

WHEN I WAS LITTLE, my grandmother, Mamere, used to read to me from a storybook about a mermaid who lived at the bottom of an alpine lake. She fell in love with a farmer who often sat by the shore, and convinced him to come live with her under the water. They were happy. They were in love. But every few months he would get lonely and homesick for something he missed from the land above the water. His cow, his farm, the meadows. He couldn't stop thinking about life back home going on without him. The mermaid really wanted to keep him there, keep him happy. So bit by bit, she would bring each part of his world down to the bottom of the lake, too, until finally she had magically transported his whole village to the deepest depths of the water. Then he had everything he ever wanted, everything he needed, everything he loved—his home, his cow, the woman of his dreams. And they stayed there together, happily ever after.

The people who live near this lake still say that if the water is clear, you can look down into it and see the tips of the church spires, the streets laid out neatly, and the perfect little cottages with red-and-white-checkered curtains fluttering in the waves that move past their windows.

I think about that story sometimes now and picture Bayou Perdu like that, the way it was before the storm. What if the waves that tore it apart had really swallowed it whole and it was still out there, perfectly preserved under the water? And we were all still out there, the way we used to be? If you looked down, you could see the diner, and Mama would be coming out with her hair pulled up and her apron on, and Mandy would be picking her up in the truck after cheerleading practice, her hair swinging in that tight ponytail. Our house would be there on Robichaux, and Mrs. Menil would be sitting out on that big front porch of the house next door, watching everyone and muttering crabbily. Mr. Ray would say, "How's yo' mama?" every time I walked past the gas station. I would be there on the dock, with my legs dangling over the side, scanning the edge of the sight line.

Then the black dots would appear on the horizon, getting bigger and bigger until you could see they were trawlers, make out the nets raised up on their sides, and finally hear the hum of the engines. We'd bring in the catch like always, and life in Bayou Perdu would continue, the way it was meant to be. We'd never have to feel lonely or homesick for the way things were. Because everything we needed would still be there, underneath the waves. We wouldn't be able to see all the way up to the surface, see the dark clouds rolling in or feel the wind so strong it could pull up a whole town by its roots and smash it to pieces. We'd still be all together. We'd still be whole. We wouldn't have to search around for those missing pieces of ourselves that can never be put back the same way again.

Before

August 2005

I AM ABOUT TO MAKE HISTORY, and not in a good way if my mother and sister are to be believed. Today, I will become the first queen in Bayou Perdu to ever put on her sash and tiara without an ounce of hair spray or a drop of makeup. Not to mention that I'm wearing jeans and white rubber boots.

"Have some *respect* for the position," my sister, Mandy, hisses at me as we're leaving the house for the Blessing. "I'm not saying you need to wear a dress. A nice pair of shorts and heels like last year's Fleet Queen wore. Just make an effort."

"I'm doing this because I'm representing the marina. And this is what we wear there," I shoot back. Mandy always wants drama. I'm not going to give it to her. "You wouldn't know because you never come to the marina to work."

"But there are going to be *photographers*. Maybe even from the *Times-Picayune*," Mama chimes in. "This isn't just about you, Evangeline. This is about the diner, too. How do you think it reflects on the diner when you don't even try?"

"Let's not forget that the Blessing of the Fleet is a religious event," Mamere counters. "It's not about what anybody is wearing."

"Evangeline looks great. Everybody get in the truck," Daddy says with finality, ending the discussion.

If you had to rank the women in the Riley household in order of likelihood to be queen of anything, the answer would be this: 1. Mama, otherwise known as Vangie Beauchamp Riley. She was on the Orange Queen Court in 1979, and although she didn't win, she is the reigning queen of the local restaurant scene, such as it is. She's the owner of Vangie's Diner, home of the best shrimp po'boys in southern Plaquemines Parish, and the place where you find out where the fish are biting. 2. Mandy, my older sister, Bayou Perdu High cheerleading cocaptain, star softball player, shoo-in for this year's Orange Queen competition. 3. Mamere, my grandmother, Evangeline Beauchamp, retired Bayou Perdu Elementary kindergarten teacher, town grandmother, beloved by all. 4. Me, Evangeline Riley, tomboy, best known for back-to-back championships in the under-sixteen fishing rodeo, French Club vice presidency, and avoidance of anything that remotely involves seeking the attention of large groups of people.

As a teenage girl in Bayou Perdu, it was probably inevitable that I would end up on a royal court sometime. I guess I should explain since that statement makes it sound like I live in a Disney movie. My home is a little like a fairy-tale land to me——a tiny, secret place that almost no one knows about; the place where Louisiana takes its last breath before plunging into the Gulf of Mexico. Barges from all over the world glide up the Mississippi every day on their way to New Orleans, passing by without even seeing us on the other side of the levee. The most beautiful birds you've ever seen — roseate spoonbills, blue herons, and snowy egrets — build their nests in our marshes in the winter and teach their babies to fly here. And sometimes when you're in the back bayou, you'll come upon something that just knocks the breath out of you, like a half-submerged old French tomb or a plantation wall from hundreds of years ago, when there were millions of acres of solid ground here before the sea swallowed it up. That's what I see. What outsiders see when they look at Bayou Perdu is this: a tiny village of two thousand; a collection of run-down houses and trailers; shrimpers, fishermen, oystermen, and orange growers struggling to make a living. Maybe we're out of touch with the modern world. Maybe we hold on to our traditions longer than we should. But we celebrate the change of every season with a festival, and for us, it's not really a party until there's a parade and a teenage girl with a crown on her head.

The Orange Queen is the ultimate royal title here. Mandy will be Orange Queen or die trying. But there's also Mardi Gras Queen, Homecoming Queen, Catfish Queen, and Shrimp and Petroleum Queen, not to be confused with the queen of *just* shrimp. Fleet Queen, which I'm about to become, is just about the least prestigious title, only slightly better than Sulfur Queen. If somebody nominates you, like the owner of the marina nominated me, you end up as a court member. You don't have to do much—just walk behind the queen and wave. Unless you're me and you happen to be the second-highest vote getter when the queen's arrested for underage drinking and is disqualified. So here I am, the most reluctant royal in the history of Bayou Perdu. The only person more shocked than me was Mandy, who never dreamed that her nonblond, considerably less attractive little sister would beat her to royal title status, even if it is about the sorriest excuse for a royal crown in town.

When we get to Our Lady of the Sea, our church and the starting point of the procession, the paparazzi Mama worried about have not arrived, but some of the other court members are there, including my best friend, Danielle. They're dressed in everything from jean shorts and sandals to sundresses. "Oh, this is just great!" Mandy shrieks. "Don't they have someone to coordinate outfits? You are the *only* one in long jeans and those stupid boots!"

"Well, then she gets an A for originality," Daddy says, winking at me.

Mandy grabs her pom-poms from the back and huffs out of the truck.

Danielle watches with me as Mandy flounces away. "She brought her pom-poms?" she asks under her breath.

I can always count on Danielle to understand my Mandy problems. "You know, in case a cheerleading emergency breaks out," I say.

"Hello, Danielle," Mama says in a cool, clipped tone. Mamere has told me not to take it too personally the way Mama treats Danielle. She says Mama's just trying to protect me. It's true Mama let Danielle live with us last year after another of her mother's "questionable decisions about men" went wrong and they ended up homeless for a few months. But if anything, Danielle's a good influence. She's more mature than me — the kid who has always had to be the grown-up in her house. I want to say that Mama's in no position to judge since we may very well have been homeless four years ago after yet another miserable shrimping season if Mamere hadn't invited us to come live with her when Grandpere died. But I don't.

Mamere comes up and gives Danielle one of her grandmotherly hugs. *"T'es parés, mes filles?"* she asks. Are you ready? We're both in French Club, so she likes to help us out by speaking French, even though her French is Cajun and not exactly right.

The Blessing of the Fleet is held at the tail end of the Shrimp Festival, right as brown-shrimp season ends and white-shrimp season begins. Truthfully, I love the Blessing. It's the last big festival of summer before school starts back, and it always comes right around my birthday, which happens to be this Friday. But I never thought I'd attend it in a big custom-made rhinestone crown with a pink bejeweled shrimp at its center.

Our parish priest starts the procession with altar boys and girls and the Knights of Columbus with their big feathered hats, red capes, sashes, and swords. When you say it, it sounds like another description from a fairy tale, too, but they're just some of the old men from the church, usually the more distinguished members of the community — Grandpere was one. Next comes my fellow monarch for this event, the King Crustacean, who is in this case Mr. Gonsales, the JV football coach. He is wearing a crown, too, but he's also got on these long red gloves that have shrimp claws instead of fingers. And then there's the queen, selected by ballot by the fishermen at the marina. Yes, that would be me, smiling behind gritted teeth.

There aren't actually too many people here at the start of the procession. It's the Catholics at this point, which in Bayou Perdu includes anyone with a French-, Italian-,

Irish-, Croatian-, Spanish-, or Vietnamese-sounding last name. This is the solemn part of the day's events. We're not so much into solemn in Bayou Perdu. We're more *laissez les bons temps rouler,* and the *rouler*-ing starts around noon.

As we walk from the church down to the harbor, more and more people join the procession and everyone is singing "Praise God from Whom All Blessings Flow." Danielle catches my eye every once in a while and tries to make me laugh. She's good at that. I almost crack. People greet me with puzzled looks, trying to figure out which one is the queen. Could it really be the girl in white rubber boots? Why on earth would any girl not put on a multitiered, bugle-bead-encrusted, ruched-bodice taffeta gown when given the opportunity? I sense I am a disappointment, even for a Fleet Queen.

The photos at the dock are about as painful as I thought they would be. I overhear comments about me like "Natural look this year" and "Good to have one of the white-boot brigade this time." My favorite is "I thought it was going to be the other Riley girl." As the shutters snap, Mr. Gonsales leans in uncomfortably close for our queen and king shots.

The crowd has swelled now. Out-of-towners are here. Lots of them. There's a TV crew. Someone says they're from France, here to document this quaint European custom that still holds on in this remote part of the U.S. The boats come parading into the docks, all decorated with flags flapping in the wind. We ride around the marina in the Vulniches' boat as the priest sprinkles holy water on each vessel he passes. When we come back, he delivers his homily, asking God to fill our fishermen's nets. This shrimping season has not been the best, he acknowledges, with Hurricanes Dennis and Arlene keeping us off the water for days. But this fall will be different, better. Of course we all know that hurricane season has barely even begun and there are a couple more brewing off the coast of Florida even as we gather here. But this homily is supposed to be uplifting. And shrimpers are nothing if not eternally optimistic. So along with King Crusty, I climb the rigging and hang a rosary from the top. My sister wanted me to do this in heels. The crowd erupts in cheers. They're impatient to do what we do best around here: eat, dance, drink beer, and eat some more.

Danielle and I have only a few minutes to hang out. Because today, queen or not, I have to work at the diner's booth. "Meet you at the boatshed at five?" she asks.

"I'm living for it," I say as I head toward the white tents and booths on the other side of the marina. This is where all the action is happening right now because this is where the food is.

America may be a melting pot, but Louisiana is a gumbo pot. The French came here for the sugar and rice plantations, and the enslaved Haitians and Africans were brought to do their labor. The Italians came to fish, and the Irish came to dig channels. The Croatians, like Daddy's mother, came to oyster back in the 1920s. The Vietnamese came here in the '70s to escape the war and work as shrimpers. Daddy says we're all mutts down here, a little of this and that race and culture all mixed together. You can have half a dozen shades of skin and textures of hair all in the same family, like we do. And each culture brought their flavors with them and poured them into the mix. So no matter what the festival is, you're going to find boudin and andouille — spicy Cajun sausage — beignets, those little fried doughnuts; étouffée; charbroiled oysters; salt-and-pepper crab; and of course, gumbo by the gallon.

Mama dashed up to Bellvoir yesterday afternoon to have a sign printed to hang over the Vangie's Diner gumbo booth: VANGIE'S DINER — MEET THE 2005 FLEET QUEEN, EVANGELINE RILEY! The plan is for me to stand under the sign, attracting customers because gumbo apparently tastes better when it's served by a queen. Mama needs to "work the crowd," and Mandy says that the cheerleaders have a mandatory meeting, but I know she's really not working because she thinks her outfit is too good to be covered up with an apron. When Byron Delacroix sees her in it, he's going to realize what an idiot he was to dump her for Jasmine Tannen. My sister is a brilliant romantic strategist. She flutters off toward the fun, a vision of blondness. That's me and my sister in a nutshell. She's light and I'm dark. She floats away, I'm anchored to the gumbo pot.

So here I am, in an apron with a sash reading FLEET QUEEN over it, latex gloves, and a head scarf with the crown on top of it. Such a good look. It's a shame those photographers are nowhere in sight.

It doesn't take long before people start to loosen up. The sun is blazing and zydeco music is drifting over from the boatshed. From my spot behind the gumbo pot, I can see a few older couples dancing. Kids sail in and out of view as they bounce in one of those inflatable castles. Traffic is picking up in my line. I ladle the gumbo and Mamere takes the money and chats people up.

"Hey, dawlin'. How's your mama?" "You bein' good?" "You hungry today?" *"Comment ça va?" "Ça va bien?"*

I can see Mama walking through the crowd. Coming up alongside me, she whispers in my ear. "You're filling the bowls too high. Two-thirds up. Tear the bread a little smaller. You can make the pieces half that size."

Mama is a good businesswoman. She's always got the bottom line in mind. I know it's hard to make any money in the restaurant business. Still, it strikes me as stingy. I wait till she walks away before starting to fill the bowls higher again.

Around four thirty, the food booth traffic is flat and Mamere goes off to the boatshed to "set for a spell." Mandy was supposed to be here to help, but of course she's not. So I'm standing by myself when this guy comes up. I can smell the mixture of sweat and beer on him before he even gets close to the table. His eyes are bloodshot and he's got this creepy smile on his face. I've never seen him before. He's not from around here. Probably a roughneck from the rigs, in town on his day off.

"You look lonely over here," he slurs.

We don't sell alcohol at the diner, so we don't usually get drunks. But I've had to deal with some unpleasant customers, so I know a few tricks. "Nope," I say casually. "I've got my gumbo to keep me company."

"I'm much better company than a pot of gumbo."

I doubt that, I want to say.

"Well, Fleet Queen, how old are you?"

My stomach tightens as I scan the area. No one close by. "Old enough to know better than to tell you how old I am," I say. My cheeks flush.

This wasn't the answer he wanted. He sneers and grunts. "Huh. Good one. What do you like to do for fun, Fleet Queen?" He leans in way too close.

Where is everyone? "Make gumbo." My voice doesn't sound as strong as I want it to.

He shakes his head. "That dudn't sound very fun to me. I have some better ideas about how to have fun." He leans in closer; the smell is nauseating.

Breathe deep. "Actually, you know what else I like to do for fun? Mixed martial arts. Black belt." This is an out-and-out lie. "And I'd be happy to show you some of my moves if you don't clear out."

The guy rolls his eyes and turns, waving me off like a fly and stumbling away.

Still a little rattled, I take off the tiara and sash and shove them in a box under the table, stand on a chair, and take down the sign. I take the money bag and shove it in my purse. There. My Cinderella moment is over. Still no Mandy. Well, I'm *not* doing the cleanup for her. I'm off to find Danielle and actually enjoy myself.

Most of the crowd is under the boatshed now, and it's getting loud. The band is from the part of Louisiana near where Mamere and Grandpere come from, what everyone calls Cajun country. They're playing "Hot Tamale Baby," and the accordion player is on fire. It's all I can do to stop myself from dancing the way I would back at home alone in my room. Wild and out of control until I'm out of breath. Zydeco and Cajun music just does something to me. Mamere says it's in my blood, even though what Grandpere played was traditional Cajun, much slower and sweeter than this. People are in that sort of trance they get in when they're dancing, feet moving lightning fast, whirling around, sweaty, unaware of anything around them but the music. I circle the edge of the crowd looking for Danielle, and as soon as I see her, I know something's wrong. And I can guess what it is.

When she reaches me, I can see she's holding back tears.

"Desiree?" I ask. She calls her mom by her first name, so I do, too.

She nods.

"Where is she?"

She points to the edge of the dance floor. Her mom, in too-short jean shorts and a bikini top, clearly wasted, is grinding up against some sketchy guy.

"I tried to get her to leave a bunch of times, but she pushed me away. She's probably going to puke any minute from all that spinning. Then he won't be so into her. I need to get her home."

It's always the same story with Danielle's mom. She's been to rehab a few times, but the recovery never seems to take. It's not even the drinking so much as it is what Danielle calls "love addiction." I've lost count of how many times Desiree moves in with some guy and drags Danielle with her. It always ends badly.

"I'll get Daddy," I say. "Want to come with me?"

She shakes her head. "I need to keep my eye on her."

I know I'll find Daddy across the way at the marina, hanging out with men drinking Bud tallnecks, telling their fish tales. "You hear? Cap'n Al caught a two-hundred-pound swordfish!"

Daddy's never one to tell tales, but he never questions the ones other fishermen tell. He's one of the guys. I find him with some of the charter captains. "What's up, baby?" he asks when I approach. I guess it's obvious something's wrong.

"Desiree. Can you help?" I know he will.

He excuses himself and comes back with me to the boatshed, where Danielle is leaning against one of the corner walls, watching her mother make out with the total stranger as the band continues to get louder and the dance floor more crowded.

Daddy comes up behind Danielle's mom and taps her on the shoulder. "Hey, darlin'. How you doin'?"

"John!" Desiree's face lights up. They were in the same class at Bayou Perdu High, along with Mama. "You wanna dance? You sure Vangie's OK with that?"

"Sure, let's dance," he says, stepping between her and the roughneck. She flops her head on Daddy's shoulder.

"Hey! I'm dancin' with her," the guy slurs.

"It's all right," Daddy says to the guy. "She's going to take a little break."

The guy shoves Daddy, but he almost topples over himself. In less than a minute, a big burly security guard is on him, holding his arm back before he can throw a punch at Daddy.

"Now, wait a second," says Desiree. "We were having a good time."

Danielle steps in. "Mama, we're going to go home now."

"I don't want to go home. I was havin' a good time."

Daddy puts his arm around her and starts to lead her out of the boatshed with Danielle trailing behind. "Let's get some fresh air. I'm going to give you a ride home," he says, and whispers to me, "Just let Mama know I'll be back soon."

I grab Danielle's hand and squeeze it as she pulls away,

leaving me feeling low as the music lifts and spirals. The couples continue to spin across the floor. This is the flip side of this fairy-tale place. Some people drink, eat, dance, and drink some more to forget. And some of them, like Danielle's mom, have a lot they want to forget.

When the song comes to an end, an announcer comes out. "Hey, folks, here in Cavalier country football season starts next week! So we'd like to bring out some members of the team and the Lady Cavaliers to lead us in this next dance!"

So this is why Mandy didn't show up to clean the booth. And brought her pom-poms. She and her friends come out, doing jumps and bouncing around in front of the football players. OK, that's it. Party officially ruined for me. She never had any intention of coming to help clean up. It was all going to fall to me as usual. I am out of here. I am going to the only place where I can calm down: on the water.

Down at the docks, our family's two boats float side by side: the *Mandy* is the big trawler, the source of our income and central to our existence; the *Evangeline* is the little skiff, too small to be named, really, but Daddy did so in an attempt at fairness. The *Mandy* can get out into the deep water, but the *Evangeline* has her advantages. She's quick, nimble, and responsive. She can get in and out of the tightest spots. She's the one to pick if you want to go deep into the back bayou, the hidden places. I'd choose her anytime over the *Mandy*. And I do now.

The sun is a little softer as I head out. In front of me is the endless water, the channels leading into the back bayou where there is nothing but sky and air and water and wings, and peace comes over me. I feel like if I spend too much time off the water, I start to shrivel up. I remember trying to explain it one night at the dinner table when I was little, how I feel like the water is in me.

"Of course the water is in you," Mandy said in her know-it-all way. "Our bodies are, like, eighty percent water."

"Nah, it's 'cause she's a mermaid," Daddy said. "I caught her in a net when she was just a little slip of a thing. Was gonna throw her back, but she was just so cute."

"I'm cuter," Mandy sniffed.

Thoughts come to me when I'm on the water. It's clear who I am out here. Not who I am compared to anyone else. Out here feels like the truth to me, the simple truth. Earth, air, sky, water. A natural rhythm to life. This is our place in the world, and I know my place in it. The exact opposite of high school, where pretty much everything and everyone feels fake all the time.

My sixteenth birthday is Friday, and school starts the Monday after that. Junior year. People keep telling me how important it is. Everyone says I can get into LSU, get a scholarship if I keep my grades up and do well on the SATs.

Everything seems focused on getting out of here, and going forward means going away. And yet I feel this tug to stay, help Daddy on the boat. Shrimping is no way to make a living, he says. I can help more if I get an education and make money doing something else. What is the something else? The idea of sitting in an office all day feels like dying to me. I'll never do that. But what's the answer?

I head to a place Daddy and I call Bayou Valse d'Oiseau — Bird's Waltz Bayou. It's hidden in the middle of a bunch of islands in the back bayou, and the birds from the flyway roost here in the spring. Most of them have moved on by now, but a few herons stay year-round. I've always been convinced that Daddy and I are the only ones who know this place and there's never been anyone here before. But there's a jon boat here now, close to one of the little islands.

As I get closer, I can see a guy on the boat waving his arms over his head, like a distress signal. He didn't cut the engine in time and ended up grounded in the skinny water. Lucky for him that I showed up.

I glide in. I've never seen this guy before. I've actually never seen anyone quite like him.

There are basically three types of guys at my school. There's the jock type, the hip-hop guys who think they're really street even though they live in rural Louisiana, and the church youth group guys who are nice but boring. Each category has black guys, white guys, and Asian guys. This guy is like none of them. I mean he is Asian, and about my age. But his hair is a little long and shaggy, and he's wearing long plaid shorts, a white T-shirt, and a hat. Not a baseball hat like the jocks or a knit cap like the hip-hop guys. It's like something Grandpere would have worn in the '50s. I'm not sure what it's called—a porkpie hat?

"Well, this is awkward," he says. "I appear to be stuck. And I appear to be an idiot."

"Yep," I say. "I mean about the being stuck part. Not the idiot part."

"That's kind of you," he says. "But I'm smart enough to know how stupid it is that I did this."

He's right. Going out into unknown waters without any navigation equipment is pretty stupid.

"I usually know how to find my way around the water," he continues. "I thought I could figure out how to get back to the marina. I thought maybe there was a cut-through. But here I am. The water got skinny so quickly. I don't think I sucked in any mud, I think I'm caught in the grass."

I pull alongside him and tie on. The water here probably wouldn't come up to my waist. Our towline broke last week and I hadn't gotten a chance to replace it yet, so that's not an option. But the situation doesn't look drastic.

"I tried working the throttle in reverse but no luck," he continues.

"Why don't you pass the cooler and anything else you've got over to me to lighten the load," I say. "Then we can each take a side and see if we can rock it loose."

He passes over the cooler. And a guitar case. Interesting.

The lighter load raises the boat a little, and I slip into the water. He looks surprised. "You're not worried about the gators?"

"They're more afraid of us than we are of them," I say, trying to make myself sound tough. But he's not pretending to be tough around me, so maybe I don't have to, either. "Actually, I've never seen one back here."

He heaves himself into the water.

"Ready?" I ask. "Go gentle so you don't damage the motor, but strong, too. You just have to feel your way through it. Go with the flow, no pun intended."

We both start rocking, creating gentle waves.

"So you're not from around here?" I ask over the side of the boat.

"I came down for the festival. My cousins live here. The Trans, do you know them?"

I know everyone in Bayou Perdu. Hip Tran is on the football team, so he's more or less a minor deity. "Yeah, I know them," I say. "Their boat slip is near ours. Where do you live?"

"Up in St. Bernard," he says.

I can feel the weeds starting to loosen. We got the rhythm going easily. This is working.

"How did you end up all the way out here?" I want to know how he found my unfindable place.

"Kind of a long story. Let's just say there was some

drama and I wanted to get away for a while. I borrowed my cousin's boat. Is it still borrowing if you don't ask? I guess I kind of stole it. I mean, I'm going to bring it back if we can get it loose. How about you? How did you end up all the way out here?"

We continue to rock.

"My dad and I come here a lot. It's a great place to catch reds. And it's on the flyway. You should see it in the springtime. There must be ten thousand birds back here. And the way they move together, it looks like a dance." I tell him our name for this place.

A look comes over his face. A smile and a kind of dreamy look. "Bird's Waltz Bayou," he repeats. "That would be a great song name. 'The Ballad of Bird's Waltz Bayou.'"

"So do you write songs?"

"Very poorly."

"I noticed the guitar."

"I play better than I write. Do you play anything?"

"I can play the accordion a little. And I sing. What kind of music do you play?"

He tells me about the blues. John Lee Hooker. Howlin' Wolf. Bukka White. We're rocking the boat long enough for him to give me an abbreviated history of Creole music and Dixieland, swamp pop and zydeco, how each rhythm got mixed in with the others like the flavors in a gumbo pot. I'm watching him talk about it, get excited about it, show that he's excited about it, which is not something that most guys do. Not something I do. Sometimes I think I spend so much time trying to avoid drama that I don't let myself get excited about anything. But like Mamere always says, you've got to have some fight to you. The way I do when there's a forty-pound yellowfin on the other end of the line.

I feel the prop come loose from the weeds and the boat lurches free. "Yes!" he shouts. "We did it!" He starts laughing. A kind of uninhibited, overjoyed laugh. "You have no idea what was going through my head. I was picturing myself sleeping out here. And then the buzzards coming in the morning after I died of dehydration. I have a very active imagination."

We push the boat back a little to where I know the water is slightly deeper. He hurls himself over the side of the boat and pulls me up, and I'm suddenly very conscious of the fact that I look like a drowned rat.

"I think I better be getting back now," he says. "Then again, I have no idea how to get back, so . . ."

"You can follow me. It's not far. You just have to know where you're going."

"This has been more fun than I thought getting lost and running a boat aground could be. So, this is kind of a weird question. But did I see you earlier today in a crown? With a pink rhinestone shrimp on it?"

I can feel the color rising in my cheeks. "Uh, yeah. That was me. I mean, it's not really *me,* me. The real queen got caught with an open container, so I had to step in. It's complicated."

"You are just coming to the rescue all over the place today, aren't you?" he jokes. "You're like some kind of superhero. With a crown instead of a cape."

"Yeah, that's me. Able to climb rigging and rescue stranded boaters. All without dropping my shrimp crown."

"Can you, like, breathe for extended periods of time underwater?"

"No, but I do make a good gumbo."

"Gumbo Girl!" he says. "I've seen you in Marvel comics, right?"

"Yes, I battle the evil Captain Crawfish."

"By biting his head off and boiling him in Zatarain's."

"And that's just in volume one. You should see what I do to Oyster Man in volume two."

"Tabasco. Right to the eyeballs," he says, and pretends to squeeze a bottle of hot sauce. "Wait, do oysters even have eyes?"

"Not when I'm done with them."

Then we say nothing. I feel myself relaxing in the silence between us like it's cool water.

"Seriously, though," he says. "I really appreciate it. This whole embarrassing incident could have turned out so much worse."

"Don't worry. Your secret is safe with me."

He follows me up the channel as the sun is starting to set, and I turn around every once in a while to see if he's still there. He's still there.

We get back to the marina, and he ties up at the Trans' slip and comes over to ours. The music from the boatshed seems louder now. "Uh-oh," he says. "I see Hip. It looks like he's coming this way. He doesn't look happy." He hesitates. "I don't even know your name. I'm pretty sure it's not Gumbo Girl. I'm Tru."

"I'm Evangeline."

"Like in the poem."

Everyone in Louisiana knows about Evangeline, the heroine of the Longfellow poem about the Acadians who fled Canada and ended up here in Louisiana, becoming known as Cajuns. There's a parish named after her, a state park, the Evangeline Oak in St. Martinville, songs, restaurants. My family has had at least one Evangeline in every generation for a hundred years, including me, Mama, and Mamere. Where Mamere grew up in St. Martin Parish, if you go to any graveyard, you'll find about a hundred dead Evangelines. But the story is one of those boring history things that most kids just suffer through.

"You remember the poem?" I hear my voice getting high and Mandy-ish, but I don't know how to stop it.

"'The fairest of all the maidens was Evangeline.'" He pauses. "Or something like that. Yeah, you know, Louisiana History in seventh grade? We take that in St. Bernard, too."

"I think a lot of people in my school catch up on their sleep during that class," I say.

"I come down here kind of a lot," he says. "So maybe I'll see you again?"

"I'm not going anywhere. You know where to find me," I say.

"Just look for the girl in a shrimp crown?" he asks. "Thanks again, Evangeline," he adds as he's walking away, looking over his shoulder. He waves. Turns around. Turns back to me. Waves again. Picks up his pace as Hip gets closer. They meet and I can see from here that Hip is making angry hand gestures. He doesn't turn around again.

The next day is my idea of a perfect day. I leave home with Daddy at safe light, going out into the marsh in the *Evangeline,* gliding up the channels between the canebrakes. There's no noise except the sound of the outboard and just a little rustle of the wind and the water through the tall grass. The light in the east filters up slowly, like the petals of a flower opening, and the shadows take shape. The first pelicans fly in formation above us, and closer, you can hear a wing flap or a swish in the water, see the sleek movement of a nutria or a gator just beneath the surface. We reach the mudflats and start reeling in reds effortlessly, and then head home before the sun gets too high, passing the guys by the side of the marsh in folding chairs with their rods propped up and their beer cans already popped open. When we get back home, Kendra comes over and we sit on opposite sides of the hammock between two satsuma trees in the orange grove that Grandpere planted when he retired. Our heads are on the ends and our feet are in the middle, doing what we do best, "visiting" as her mama calls it.

"I'm actually glad I couldn't get the day off work," says Kendra. "Because you in a crown? That's a sight you just can't unsee." She covers her eyes. "Agh! My eyes! They're burning."

"Well, get ready, because the shrimp crown is coming your way. I don't want it in my room. I'm going to hide it under your pillow," I say.

"I'm going to have nightmares," she says. "Can you imagine me in a crown? I'd look like a French Quarter drag queen."

Kendra is five foot eleven and the star of the varsity basketball team. It is safe to say she will never wear a crown. A championship ring, perhaps, but not a crown.

Kendra and I have kind of an unlikely friendship. She's black and I'm white, mostly. She's an athlete and I'm pretty much a nerd. But when she was little, Mamere used to watch her after school, so we always played together. When we got old enough to mind ourselves, we'd still walk home together after school. She comes over without even calling and doesn't knock before coming in. I always say she's the sister I always wished I had. Mandy loves that.

We get to the part of the day when I went out on the water and met that guy, Tru. I rush through the story and end with "Anyway, he lives in St. Bernard."

She gives me one of her skeptical looks, with one eyebrow raised. "Mmm-hmm."

"What?"

"There's something different about the way you told that story."

"What?"

"You like him."

"I don't even know him."

"So? You like him. Maybe this is going to be the year."

"What year?"

"The year you become a woman," she jokes. I kick her in the shin. "Just playin' with you. The year somebody comes in and sweeps you off your feet."

I am not the kind of girl who has crushes all the time. When you spend as much time around guys as I do at the marina, there's not a whole lot of mystery there. "OK, maybe. I'm interested. A little. Sort of. Don't say anything to anyone," I beg.

"Come on. Who would I tell?"

We don't have any of the same friends at school, so it makes it easier for us to tell each other anything. Nothing we say to each other ever gets around, and that's big. "So if this is going to be the year of love for me, what's it going to be for you?"

"The year of victory," she says with a laugh. I know she's imagining a state championship, which will put her on the radar of college scouts. We both sit back and dream a little as a goldfinch's song carries through the breeze, lightly scented with orange blossom.

The night before my birthday, Mamere and I are in her room. She is one of those real old-fashioned Cajun ladies who keeps her hair long, braided, and piled on her head in a bun. She says that in her day, a woman's hair was her crowning glory and she would only let it down and show it off to her husband at night. Sometimes when I was little, I'd catch sight of her hair down, like in the morning when Mama would send me over to borrow a cup of milk or something and Mamere was still in her nightgown. It was like seeing a real live mermaid or something, breathtaking and rare. Now that we live together, she lets me brush it for her at night. It falls well below her shoulders. It looks like a waterfall in moonlight, silver and shining, long and flowing. I am brushing her hair, and I guess I'm humming because she says, "You've got something good inside of you that's trying to get out."

She has a way of saying things that I'm never sure if it's her English or just her way of talking.

"It's my birthday tomorrow."

"Sweet sixteen," she says. "I was your age when I met your grandfather."

She tells me about when she was a girl my age, back in St. Martinville, and they used to have the *fais do-do* on Saturday nights. The girls would be on one side of the room and the boys on the other. There were some boys who were bold, as she put it, and they'd come up and ask any girl to dance. But Grandpere was different. He waited a long time and got to know her. He walked her home from school and carried her books and courted her. He serenaded her with his accordion, a song he made up. There's a famous Cajun dance song called the "Evangeline Special." But he thought it was too fast, so he created a sweet, slow one, Mamere told me. He called it the "Sweet Evangeline Waltz."

"You're pretty special, Mamere," I say. "To have a song named after you."

"I got *you* named after me, baby girl," she says. "Nothin' better than that."

"Do things really change when you're sixteen?" I ask. "I mean, is there something magical about that age? Other than being able to drive?"

She gets a kind of misty, kind of sad look in her eyes. "It's a time to be careful, but not too careful. Reckless, but not too reckless. You realize that you have the power to do anything. It's your choice. Maybe that's what makes it magical. When you're my age, you're going to look back on this time as the happiest of your life."

She hums a little tune. I rest my head on her shoulder, wondering when this magical life of mine is going to begin.

The Storm

MY SIXTEENTH BIRTHDAY starts with breakfast in bed: *pain perdu* — New Orleans French toast — with homemade marmalade and a cloud of uncertainty on the side. Something is nagging at me, like a pebble in my shoe. I would automatically think it was Mandy, but she's not here — she went off to the diner with Mama first thing. Daddy's been out shrimping all night and won't be back until the evening. It's only Mamere and me at home.

She's sitting on the porch staring off toward the levee when I come out on my way to pick up my schedule for school, which starts Monday. "There's a bad storm coming. Listen. No birds. That's what happened before Camille."

I vaguely remember a news report yesterday afternoon about yet another hurricane somewhere in Florida.

"Even the crickets. No crickets. Hear that?"

All I can hear are the eighteen-wheelers rumbling down Highway 23. "Sure, Mamere. Thanks for breakfast." I kiss her good-bye, put in my earbuds, turn on my music, and walk off to school. Mamere has all these Cajun folk beliefs, like hens not laying eggs and cows not giving milk before a storm, and dogs howling when they see death coming down the road. There's something to it, I know. I've noticed the pelicans disappearing before a big storm. But I've got too much other stuff on my mind to worry about it right now.

I think back to my conversation in the hammock. Maybe Kendra's right. Maybe I really am ready for love. More than a sloppy kiss at a party or an awkward slow dance. Something real. An image drifts into my mind. Tru's smile.

The image takes me so far away, I practically step out into the road without looking, an eighteen-wheeler whizzing by, its horn blasting me back to reality.

School has that first-day-back energy, even though we're just picking up schedules and classes don't start until Monday. There are people with new shoes, new haircuts, summer tans, braces finally removed. No one is in a uniform, and we can all see what we'd wear if we ever had the choice. I wave as I see Danielle, looking, as usual, like she's wearing the clothes she slept in, a style I like but that my mother and sister judge her for. She's carrying a balloon and something wrapped in tinfoil.

She runs up to me. *"Happy birthday to you, happy birthday to you. Happy birthday, dear Evangeline. Happy birthday to you,"* she sings in a goofy voice.

"Oh, thanks, you always know how to publicly embarrass me!" I say, unwrapping the tinfoil to find a giant cookie with a smiley face of chocolate icing.

"It's from a roll of cookie dough from the freezer section of the grocery store," she says. "I peeled off the wrapping all by myself." We have an ongoing joke about my insistence on cooking from scratch and her reliance on food from boxes.

"I can tell that. Thank you! It's beautiful. Mmm, just smell the preservatives!" I say. The balloon suddenly pops with a bang.

"I don't think I got my twenty cents' worth out of that balloon." Danielle shrugs. "Sorry about that. Oh, and I almost forgot this." She pulls something wrapped in newspaper from her purse. "Your present!"

I unwrap it, revealing a skein of cotton yarn.

"For your new hobby!"

I've taken up knitting to pass the downtime in the summer when I'm out shrimping with Daddy. "Just enough to make you something for *your* birthday." I pass her a gooey piece of cookie. "Everything OK?"

"OK," she says. "She got up in time for the bus this morning."

"That's a good sign." Desiree started a new job at the Home Depot outside Bellvoir, and Danielle has been holding her breath that it works out so they'll have some steady income.

"Have you seen Evan LaSalle's buzz cut?" she says, changing the subject. I get it. Sometimes she just wants to forget about it for a while.

We get in line in the gym to register, making small talk. Will Amber actually come talk to us? She completely dumped us at the beginning of the summer when she started going out with Taylor. Danielle and I don't really belong to any group. We just ease in and out of the little clusters of people. Not outcasts, but not popular, like Mandy and her friends, who I can see from across the gym. Sort of in the middle, like Kaye Pham and Elly Reynolds, who are standing in front of us. There's nothing particularly wrong about them, but nothing particularly right, either.

"I just had this weird feeling," I overhear Kaye saying. "When he said he had boat trouble when we were at the Blessing. I just had this feeling he was with someone else."

"Don't be paranoid," says Elly. "It's a turnoff. You're not going to get much further if you start acting needy. Did he say he'd call you?"

"No, he doesn't have a phone. But he's on JD's soccer

team. So I thought maybe I would get a ride up with Hip next time they're having a game."

"I'll come with you," Elly says. "That makes it seem less like you're stalking him."

"I'm not stalking him!" Kaye exclaims. "He could have said no when Hip suggested we meet."

"I'm just kidding!" says Elly. "It's going to be so cool when you get to vote for him on *American Idol*!"

A sick feeling trickles through me. Because I know who they are talking about: Tru. And he *was* with someone else. He was with me. I start to blush. Because I had been thinking for the past few days — more often than I'd like to admit — that maybe he liked me. Maybe there was something there. But he came down here to go out with Kaye Pham.

The conversation goes on, speculating on why he could have been gone for so long and whether he seemed as interested when he came back. I stand there in silent misery until they finally get their schedules and move away.

"What's up?" says Danielle when we've got ours. "You look like you're going to puke. Was it my cookie?"

"The guy I told you about the other day," I say frantically. "From the Blessing? From St. Bernard? That's who they were talking about. He's going out with Kaye."

"I thought you said he was cool."

"He was. I thought he was."

"Clearly you need to rethink that."

"Why? There's nothing really wrong with Kaye. I could sort of see how he'd like her."

"She's just so ordinary," says Danielle.

"So am I."

"Yeah, right," says Danielle. "Superstar badass fishing champion. Fleet Queen."

But that conversation becomes a black cloud hovering around me all day. So far, being sixteen is not off to a great start.

Daddy wears a serious expression as he sits down at the dinner table for my birthday dinner. "Just got off the phone with Cal," he says. "They're saying the hurricane that was supposed to hit the Panhandle is moving west. They're projecting a Category Three."

Mama looks annoyed, flips on the TV, and goes straight to the Weather Channel.

Projected to make landfall sometime between Sunday night and Monday morning as far west as the Mississippi-Louisiana border.

Mandy rolls her eyes. "Yeah, right."

"This one's no joke," says Mamere. There's a seriousness in her voice. The same way she sounded this morning when she was talking about the birds. When Mamere sounds like that, everyone listens. "We need to go."

Mama does that thing she does when she thinks Mamere

is overreacting. Her voice turns all high and sweet. "Mama, let's wait and see. It's Evangeline's birthday. We don't need to think about it until tomorrow."

"Sitting on I-10 for eighteen hours Sunday, you're gonna be wishin' you thought about it tonight," Mamere warns.

"I think Mamere's right. I think we're going to need to go," Daddy says firmly. This is a surprise. Leaving means losing money. Losing money is what he always avoids. His face is grim. I know he's serious.

We're not *leavers*. We're certainly not the type to leave early. I can't believe we're even talking about this. It's my birthday. We haven't had cake yet.

"If we're gonna go, we should do it right," Daddy continues. "We should get out of here by afternoon tomorrow if we're going to beat the traffic."

Mama sighs and frowns. "We'll never find a place in Baton Rouge. Everything'll be booked."

Mamere tilts her head back like she always does when she knows she's about to say something that Mama won't like. It's like she's trying to get some distance between herself and the words that she knows Mama will hurl at her. "There's no reason on earth we can't stay by your cousin Kenny. Five bedrooms in that house."

Mamere's three sisters still live in and around St. Martinville—Tante Sadie, Tante Marie, and Tante Fifi. Most of their kids stayed in the area, but my mom's cousin Kenny is a lawyer in Baton Rouge and we used to stay with him whenever we did evacuate. Mama hates it, though. She doesn't like his wife and she feels poor in his house. She shakes her head. "I'm not showing up at that woman's house so she can lord her money over me. I'd rather sleep in the car."

"What about Fifi's house, then? I'd like to see my sister."

Tante Fifi has a little house by herself in St. Martinville. I've always loved to go there because I get to see the Evangeline Oak, this beautiful, noble, hundreds-of-years-old oak tree that's supposed to be the place where the girl who inspired the poem "Evangeline" met her true love, Gabriel. We would go there when I was little, and Grandpere used to say, "You're pretty special, your Mamere and you. You got a tree named after you." I love St. Martinville, so if we have to go there, it wouldn't be so bad. It's only a few hours away. But Mama is digging in.

"No. If Baton Rouge evacuates, too, Kenny will end up at Fifi's. Let's just go to a hotel."

"Hotels cost money," says Mamere.

Mama glares at her. "I know that, Mama. But I'd rather drive all the way to Cel's than end up packed in with Kenny and that wife of his."

Mama's sister, my aunt Cel, went to LSU and never came back to Bayou Perdu. She got a job in the accounting department of this fast-food chain in New Orleans, and when they relocated to Atlanta in the '80s, she went, too.

Now she's a bigwig vice president of something. She was

married, but she and Uncle Jim got divorced a long time ago. Her daughter, Ami, lives in Washington, D.C. now.

The conversation goes back and forth. Whether to go. If we go, when do we go, where do we go? Is it worth it? Is it necessary? It's an expense we can't really afford right now.

"Wait a second," says Mamere. "Aren't we forgetting something?" She tilts her head toward me.

Mama goes in the kitchen and comes back a few minutes later with a glowing cake. *"Happy birthday to you, happy birthday to you. Happy birthday, dear Evangeline. Happy birthday to you,"* they sing. I huff out the candles, and there are a few halfhearted claps.

Mamere slides the presents across the table and I open them halfheartedly, too. A flip phone. I can't believe it. Kendra has one, but Danielle doesn't. Mandy has a phone, but she had to earn it working at the diner. I know it's a stretch financially for my parents. I know exactly how many pounds of shrimp we had to sell to get that phone. My arms practically feel sore remembering hauling all those shrimp.

"You worked real hard this summer, baby," Daddy says. "You deserve it."

I get up and hug both of them. "Thank you," I say. "This means a lot to me." It makes me feel more like I'm on par with Mandy, who gives me a compact with a bunch of different kinds of eye shadow and blush in it.

"Just try it," she says defensively. "That's all I ask."

It's just like her to give me something *she* would like.

But she did get me something. She's trying, I guess. "I will," I say. "Maybe just in the bathroom. With the door closed."

Mamere has given me her copy of *Evangeline,* the family heirloom that I've always loved, with the beautiful gold-leaf letters on the front and the woodblock illustrations. "For a girl who's got a poem named after her," she says.

I grasp her hand. *"Merci bien,"* I say. "I've always wanted this." I know it's a signal that she thinks I'm really a grown-up now.

After dinner, I listen as Mama calls a million places between Mississippi and Florida looking for a hotel room. "None available? Thanks, bye. Dammit. Yes, do you have any rooms? Nothing. OK, good-bye. Unbelievable. The whole state of Alabama is already sold out." Around eleven, she finally finds a hotel in some place called Bainbridge, Georgia, that still has rooms and free continental breakfast. It's about five hours away if we beat the traffic. Double that time if we don't. So if we leave tomorrow after we finish lunch service, we should be OK. Unless things change, we're going. But we could wake up tomorrow and the hurricane could be headed to Texas. That happens all the time.

Before bed, I'm starting on a scarf with my new skein of yarn from Danielle when Mandy stands in my door in her sweatpants, musing. "Missing the first day of school is not bad," she says. "What would be really bad is if this happened next weekend. It's the senior ring dance and the Orange Queen court selection. If it's bad and the electricity

41

is still down then, they'll have to postpone it." She is deep in thought. I'm pretty sure she's thinking about whether her tan will last that long or if the delay will mean she's going to have to go up to the tanning salon in Bellvoir to refresh it.

"Do you know anything about Hip Tran?" I ask.

"Why? Do you like him?"

I give her my *Seriously?* look. "Do you know anything about his family?"

"Why are you asking me all these weird questions?" She comes and sits on the bed, more interested in me than usual.

"Nothing. I just met his cousin."

"Is he a football player?"

"I don't think so. He lives in St. Bernard."

"Oh, so you're doing that thing," she says. "Being interested in someone out of town so people think you have a boyfriend, but you don't really."

"I'm not doing *anything,* Mandy. I just asked a question."

"Long-distance relationships don't work, Evangeline," she warns. "Trust me."

And so ends another very useful exchange with my sister. Head on pillow. Pebble in shoe. No sleep.

Everyone is glued to the TV at the diner in the morning. Projected landfall is New Orleans, with sustained winds of over 115 miles an hour. There's a big white swirl on the screen, big enough to fill up the whole Gulf of Mexico. By midmorning they're calling it Hurricane Katrina. It's now a Category 5, the weatherman says. What if a Category 5 hurricane hits New Orleans? he asks. Devastation. The levees might not hold. Same things they always say. The things that never happen. Blah, blah, blah.

The announcer ticks down the list of things you should have to prepare for the hurricane: batteries, bottled water, matches, your medicine. So far, evacuation is voluntary. That means most people won't.

"I heard that it's supposed to make landfall right here. I mean right here," says a man at the counter, probably on his way out from the refinery down the road. He taps his finger hard on the counter. "This is ground zero."

"I heard it was s'posed to hit Mississippi," says Bill, one of the truckers who's in here all the time.

Mr. Kovich, the sheriff's deputy, comes in at around ten, looking serious but with a bit of a swagger. He plants himself at the counter, puts his elbow down, and tips his hat. "Ms. Riley."

"What's the word, Tony?" Mama asks.

"Mandatory evacuation. The parish president is about to announce it."

All the men at the counter look at him. A few groan.

"Oh, come on, Tony. Mandatory?"

"Could be Category Five. Everybody out."

"They just want to scare us," says Mr. Porter, who works at the processing plant. It's his day off, and he always comes for breakfast on Saturday. "It's because of the law-suits. If they don't warn you and somethin' happens, they're screwed."

"At least we'll get the day off work," says his wife, Tammy.

"I don't work, I don't get paid," says Mama, sliding a plate of eggs to them across the counter. I hate it when she says stuff like that. It makes her sound so bitter.

"I got nowhere to go. Gotta pay for a hotel. An' my cats throw up every time I get them in the car," says Mr. Landry, the mail carrier.

"You could leave them here and leave food for them," I suggest.

"I done that last time. Didn't see Puddy again for two months."

I have to hold in a laugh. It's funny to see a two-hundred-pound, tough-looking man talk about his cat like that.

Back in the kitchen, Mamere's got the radio on. Mostly a traffic report. I-10 eastbound is still moving; 1-10 westbound to Baton Rouge is worse. The announcers are joking about it. They're offering free Saints game tickets to whoever calls in with the best rant about the traffic — a rhyme or a poem or a song, no profanity, please.

After lunch the last of the stragglers are sitting at the counter, eyes glued to the TV. Mama's in the kitchen clean-ing out the fridge and tossing food in the Dumpster out back. "Damn waste," she mutters.

At three o'clock, I swing the CLOSED sign around on the door of the diner, check the lock, and help Mama, Mandy, and Mamere carry out the coolers of food that we take home.

Everybody here knows the evacuation drill. Pull the cords out of all the electrical outlets. Get everything up off the floor, into the cabinets or on top of a table. Put the generator up in the very top of the closet — that's what you'll need the most if the power lines come down and the lights don't go back on for a week. Throw out anything perishable from the fridge. Board up the windows: I hold the boards; Daddy nails them in. Then we go next door to Mrs. Menil's house to do hers. She's sitting out in her chair, as always.

"All this fuss," she shouts, not realizing how loud she is because she's hard of hearing now. She bats her hand as if she's swatting away a fly.

"Is Delbert on his way?" Daddy asks. Delbert is her son, a big fancy lawyer in New Orleans who still comes to see her almost every week and always tries to get her to move up there.

"I told him not to, but he's on his way. Taking me to Lake Charles, for God's sake. A lot of fuss, if you ask me. I've seen my share of hurricanes in my day. Not but two worth getting up and leaving for. Betsy and Camille."

"You enjoy your time with Delbert," says Daddy, patting her on the arm. "Think of it as a vacation."

"Who goes to Lake Charles on vacation?" Mrs. Menil

growls. "If he was taking me on a cruise, that would be something."

She's still grumbling as we walk down the porch steps and wave good-bye.

Back home, I use my new phone for the first time to call Danielle. "Hey!" I chirp at her. "I'm calling from my new phone."

"Great," she says. "I'm answering from our old landline."

"So, what are you guys going to do?"

"I don't know," she says. "Desiree's at work."

"You heard it's mandatory evacuation, right?"

"Yeah," says Danielle. "But not *mandatory,* mandatory, right?"

"I think that's what *mandatory* means," I say. "You know, *mandatory.*"

"But it's not mandatory up in Bellvoir, is it? I mean, if we leave and the store's still open, she's going to lose this job. And she just got it."

Of course I didn't think about that. Never mind the fact that they don't have a car or any money to pay for a hotel. Of course she's worried about Desiree's job.

"I'm sure if it's mandatory, they'll close," I say.

"I guess," she says. She sounds worried.

"We have a hotel room. Do you want me to ask if you guys can come with us?"

"No," says Danielle. "I don't want to impose. We wouldn't fit in the truck anyway."

"Maybe you could take Claudine." Claudine is Grandpere's 1979 Chevy Impala that hasn't moved from the garage in four years and probably doesn't even start.

"It's OK," she says. "We'll just stay. It'll be fine. If it's not, they'll come get us."

"You sure?"

"Yeah, I'm sure."

When I hang up, I approach Mama cautiously. "Could we wait and leave later so Danielle and Desiree can come with us? Or could they take Claudine because they don't have a car?" I know she's going to say no.

Mama gives me a look that's half guilt and half annoyance. "Claudine's not a reliable car, sweetie. They couldn't get past Bellvoir in that thing, never mind cross state lines. Don't give me that look, Evangeline. You know I'm sorry for Danielle, but I can't be responsible for her. They've got buses that will pick people up and take them to a shelter. She should call the parish office and get scheduled for a pickup."

I call Danielle back. "There are buses that will pick you up and take you to a shelter," I tell her.

"OK," she says. "I guess we'll just do that."

"I'll call you from wherever it is we're going. On my new phone."

"Don't rub it in," she says.

I call Kendra. On my new phone. She answers on her phone that she has had since she was thirteen.

"Where are you?" I ask.

"You don't want to know," she says. "The same place we've been for an hour. On I-10 going to Houston to stay by Uncle Cedric."

"Is that Evangeline?" I hear her mom, Ms. Denise, say in the background. Kendra's mom is the opposite of Danielle's mom. She's a nurse at the navy base up in Bellvoir, and she's what Mamere calls "a force of nature." Kendra *will* be getting a basketball scholarship or those poor college basketball coaches will have to deal with Ms. Denise.

"Yes, it's her, Mama," Kendra says. "What do you want?"

"Ask her what they're doing. Where they're going," Ms. Denise shouts in the background.

"Tell her we're going to Georgia," I say.

"They're going to Georgia," Kendra repeats.

"Tell her to be safe," says Ms. Denise.

"Mama, do you just want to talk to her yourself?"

We say good-bye and I finish getting ready.

In our family, we have a tradition for those rare occasions when we do evacuate. We've each got an old tackle box that we fill with our special things, the things that we'd miss the most, that we couldn't live without. Mama's got the birth certificates and insurance documents and legal stuff for the restaurant and junk like that. Daddy has our baby pictures and some things from when he was a kid. Mandy's is always changing: mostly pictures and jewelry. Mamere has her family Bible, beautiful old rosary beads, jewelry, and pictures. When I open mine, I realize it's been a while since I've added anything. My stuffed dolphin, Sleeky, that I used to always sleep with. My first-place medals from the fishing rodeo and those little newspaper clippings about them. My spelling-bee ribbons. Report cards. A picture of Mamere and Grandpere at their wedding. A response I got when I wrote to the president about protecting the marshes and barrier islands from erosion. I scan my desk and put in a few more things from my bulletin board. The *Evangeline* book Mamere gave me the other night. I pack a bag with three changes of clothes, my knitting, and a couple more books.

It's after four when we get in the truck: Mama and Daddy in the front and me, Mamere, and Mandy in the back. There's a cooler full of po'boys and soda under our feet and ten two-gallon jugs of gas in the flatbed. There's probably not a station with any gas left between here and Alabama.

The air is still, the way it always is before a hurricane, that thick, thick stillness. The sky is blue, not a cloud in sight. Mamere was right. No birds.

When Mamere comes with us, we always start the trip with Hail Marys and the Act of Contrition on the rosary beads so that if we die, we'll get into heaven because we've already said sorry for anything we did wrong. She asks the Blessed Mother to spare us from the storm.

We sail along Highway 23 for about three miles and then come to a dead stop.

Mama lets out a big sigh. "I knew this would happen. We should have left earlier," she says.

"What do you mean?" Daddy says. "You said you wanted to stay open until after lunch."

"I *had* to open this morning," she says testily. "It's not that I wanted to. We can't do without that income."

"Then why are you blaming me for not leaving earlier?"

The car goes silent.

The late afternoon passes and we've only made it over the causeway, just past Slidell. Daddy switches off the engine and we sit. I knit, read, and look out the window. Some guys are playing football in the median of the highway. A guy sets up a camp stove and starts grilling hot dogs until a highway patrolman comes over and makes him put it away. You can hear music coming from other people's rolled-down car windows. There's a steady *thump-thump-thump* of hip-hop drifting from somewhere far away. Snatches of country music closer by.

"Can I go sit outside?" Mandy whines. "Please. I'm gonna lose my mind in here. I'll be right here in the grass."

"Go ahead," Daddy growls. "I'm getting out, too."

I watch him walk up to a group of men and start talking. Mama sighs and stretches out her legs onto his part of the seat. Mamere has dozed off.

It seems like hours before we move again. I look into the

windows of passing cars to see what other people brought with them: sometimes there are big suitcases and pillows in the backseats, dogs, the occasional TV. This wild-looking tattooed couple with bright blue and red hair and all-black clothes have a parrot that hops around the front seat and a big snake that rests on the woman's neck. Must be from New Orleans.

There are Jet Skis and small boats on trailers. Some people have written messages on their rear windows, like FOLLOW ME TO TALLAHASSEE! and CATEGORY 3 PAH-TEE!

We snack out of boredom. The sandwiches have gotten soggy and the car smells of fried shrimp. It's been about six hours when we finally get to the Mississippi border, a journey that usually takes two hours. Mamere sings in French. I skim through my birthday copy of *Evangeline,* which is, to be honest, a bit dull. My favorite parts are when Longfellow describes coming to "the Bayou of Plaquemine," which I take to mean the waters around Bayou Perdu. He calls the waters "devious" and "sluggish" and the characters get lost in them, which is one of the reasons Bayou Perdu got its name. But the way he describes the trees, the boughs of the cypress meeting in a "dusky arch," the moss trailing from the trees like "banners that hang on the walls of ancient cathedrals," the moonlight gleaming on the water, is so beautiful. It takes me right out of this car and back home for a while.

We move occasionally. I stare at the snake of red blinking lights in front of me, as far as the eye can see. I come to feel like I have never been anywhere else but in this car. By three a.m., we get to the Florida Panhandle. After Pensacola, the traffic thins out a little. The license plates aren't all from Louisiana, Alabama, or Mississippi anymore. There are fields with big, black cows along the road. It doesn't feel like we're anywhere near a coast. My eyes are raw from lack of sleep, and the inside of my mouth is sticky from soda. I wish I was anywhere but in my own skin.

It's Sunday morning when we roll into the hotel in southern Georgia. It's one of those chains that are on the side of every highway. It's been almost sixteen hours since we left home. The parking lot is jammed with cars. Evacuees, I guess. Stepping out of the car, my whole body feels like it's still moving, like I'm seasick. I fall into the queen-size bed I share with Mamere and Mandy and close my eyes to try to make it stop.

When we wake up, Daddy switches on the TV to the Weather Channel. The beautiful white swirl takes up the whole space between Florida and Louisiana. It's restless. It's strengthening. But when I look at it, I still can't really imagine destruction. It looks peaceful. It's a gathering of vapors, something you can put your hand right through. When bad things happen, it seems to me, they don't announce themselves like this. They sneak up on you and catch you by surprise. They slam you from behind, like that truck that killed Danielle's dad when she was a baby.

A ticker runs across the bottom of the screen. Hurricane

Katrina upgraded to Category 4. Winds over 175 miles per hour. Expected to make landfall overnight. They cut to the mayor of New Orleans giving a press conference. "We're facing the storm most of us have feared," he says. There's a mandatory evacuation in place for New Orleans. For the first time, I start to get scared. I step out into the hallway and call Danielle. With my new phone. She picks up.

"You're still there?"

"Yeah, still here," she says.

"You really need to leave," I say. "Aren't you getting that bus that's going to evacuate people?"

"I guess so," she says with only a slight trace of concern in her voice. "Desiree's still sleeping. I'll wake her up."

"Promise me you'll get the bus. Just call the parish office. I bet they'll come pick you up."

"OK. I will."

There's something about the way she says it that makes me not believe her.

The hotel lobby is crowded, bustling even. There are all different kinds of people: some families who look working class like us, some who look wealthier. Most look tired and annoyed. There's a feeling I can't quite describe. Not excited, but there's a sense of anticipation in the air. We're all waiting for the same thing.

"Y'all from the Gulf?" a man in the lobby asks. Daddy nods. It's strange how it's "the Gulf" now instead of Louisiana, Mississippi, and Alabama.

"We're from Pascagoula. Took us ten hours to get here."

"Took us sixteen from south Plaquemines."

People all around us ease into the conversation.

"We're from Slidell. Shoulda gone west. The traffic couldn'ta been that bad."

"No, my sister went to Houston and it took nineteen hours," another woman says.

Traffic is the great equalizer.

After lunch, it's cloudy and gray. Back in the room, Daddy turns on the Weather Channel again. "Expect devastating damage," says the reporter, who's standing in front of a casino in Biloxi wearing a blue jacket. It's not even raining yet. We can hear muffled voices and the sound of football games on TV through the wall, the smell of smoke seeping in although it's a nonsmoking hotel. The interesting part that comes with being in a hotel is wearing off. Daddy flicks back and forth between the Weather Channel and CNN all day. The hurricane will make landfall overnight, they say. I sleep well on the cushy hotel-room pillow.

I wake up to the sound of Daddy turning on the TV. A little gray light is coming in through the heavy curtains. Images of trees being whipped by the wind, water surging over a seawall somewhere, flash across the screen. *Hurricane Katrina made landfall this morning at 6:10 a.m. just east of Empire, Louisiana.* Just east of Empire, Louisiana, is just south of Bayou Perdu.

Thirty-foot storm surge. I try to imagine what that

would look like. The ceilings in our house are about eight feet high. So four times that. A sick fear spreads over me. *Unprecedented. Levee breach. A second landfall over St. Bernard Parish.*

This is bad. This is really bad.

"Why don't you all take Mamere to breakfast?" Mama says with that voice she uses when she wants to show that she can cope. "Go get something to eat. Daddy and I'll stay here and watch." Her eyes look hollow.

When I'm putting on my clothes, I feel my legs shaking. It's like that knowledge, those words, are trying to break into me and I'm mustering all my strength to keep them out. I whip out my phone and try Danielle. She doesn't answer, but it's just because she's gone. At one of those shelters. She must be.

This morning, the feeling in the lobby is different. People look stunned, tired. All that energy that bounced between people yesterday has gone. It's turned into something heavy and black that looks like it's weighing people down: their heads are bowed, their shoulders slumped. We go through the line silently and get a table near the window, watching sheets of rain pour down on the parking lot. I eavesdrop on the people around us.

"Have you heard from anyone yet?"

"No cell service down there."

"I'm sure they got to Houston. I'm sure they left in time."

"Last time I talked to her, she said they was gonna ride it out. I hope she came to her senses."

An old man in a plaid shirt at the next table catches Mamere's eye. "Where you from?"

"Plaquemines."

"That can't be good," he says, shaking his head. "It's underwater. All underwater. St. Bernard. Even Jefferson Parish."

The man at the next table reaches out and pats Mamere on the back. "Good luck. God be with you."

We get up and leave our breakfast half-eaten on the table. On the way back to the room, it's like everyone's avoiding eye contact with everyone else. Because we don't want to see what's in other people's eyes right now. Because if you see what's in their eyes, you know you have to be scared, too.

Back in the room, Daddy's still perched on the edge of the bed, the curtains closed to the rain. We huddle around the TV. Reports from the hard-hit areas are starting to come in. A few hours later, they announce that the levees in New Orleans have been breached.

The day is a blur. Daddy tries to get through to the sheriff's department, but there's no response. I am sick, sick to my stomach wondering where Danielle is. Mandy is on the phone constantly. "I told you to get off that phone," says Mama. "You're payin' if you go over your minutes."

"Byron texted me. Can you believe that? I wish I could send it to Jasmine so that she would know," says Mandy.

I want to punch her in the face. My best friend could be dying out there, and I have no way of knowing. I call Kendra and tell her that I'm afraid about Danielle.

"She's going to be OK," she says. "They wouldn't have let anybody stay there." I didn't realize how much I needed someone to say that, even though there's no way to know if it's true.

By the early afternoon, we hear that St. Bernard Parish is under ten feet of water. But no one ever says anything about Bayou Perdu. Like we're not important enough to mention.

Tuesday morning the hotel feels like a cage full of angry, hungry animals. That feeling of us all being in it together and helping each other out is gone now. It's every man for himself.

The next couple of days are spent glued to the TV. The words the announcers use to describe the scene "all across the Gulf Coast" feel intentionally cruel: *decimated, destroyed, annihilated, swept from the map, obliterated, pounded, wiped off the face of the earth. Catastrophic.* Reporters are standing in piles of rubble. New Orleans is a bowl filling with water. Coffins are floating by. People are wading in waist-deep water down Canal Street, pushing shopping carts full of stuff. People are dying in the Superdome.

I'm hardly listening, but then I hear them mention that the southern part of Plaquemines Parish "has become part of the Gulf of Mexico." It's like someone pulled a rope tight around my middle and yanked it. I picture our house like it's made from sugar, dissolving as the water licks its walls.

Daddy finally gets through to the sheriff's department. We hear him say they're going around in airboats rescuing people. Forty people somehow made it to the choir loft in the Church of Christ, and the sheriff's department went in and got them out. That's what they're focusing on now. Rescuing people and animals. He doesn't have time to say more now. "Please," I plead with Daddy. "Please ask about Danielle."

"Listen, Cal," he says. "Desiree Watts and her daughter. Were they there? Have you seen them? . . . Uh-huh. OK."

He hangs up and shakes his head, but tries to be reassuring. "They weren't there, but they could have gotten one of the buses out. They're going house to house now. I'm sure they're all right."

"Nobody is sure they're all right!" I shout. "They should have come with us. We should have given them the car."

"Evangeline," says Mama in a calm tone, "we know you're worried about them. We're all worried about them."

A surge of anger overtakes me. "If you were worried about them, you would have let them take Claudine," I nearly spit at her.

"That's not fair to your mother. Claudine doesn't even turn over most of the time," says Daddy.

I feel like I'm going to explode. "My best friend could be

dead, and we didn't help her!" I slam out the door and head to the lobby.

There's a line to use the "free Internet access" computers there, and the people in it are impatient. There's a guy who has apparently been hogging the computer for a while. A guy in an LSU sweatshirt taps him on the shoulder. "You know, there are a lot of people waiting for the computer."

The guy looks over his shoulder, then goes back to what he's doing.

The guy in the LSU sweatshirt groans loudly and turns to everyone else waiting, trying to make eye contact so we'll join in his outrage. "You're not the only person here who needs information!" he shouts at the computer hog. "You're so selfish! I'm going to get a manager."

While he's gone, the computer hog leaves and someone else takes the LSU guy's place in line.

I wait for an hour and twenty minutes before it's my turn. I log in and go straight to the *Times-Picayune* website. There's a whole message board for people looking for news, for family, for friends. I click on the Plaquemines Parish page. Some of the messages have a person's name and a question mark. There are posts like *Looking for Adrienne Baptise* or *Checking on Orleans Ave.* On the second page of the board, I see the heading *Bayou Perdu.* A guy whose family owns a big orange grove north of town found some pictures taken from a helicopter and posted them in his message.

You can only see the top of the levee, the roof of our school. School buses, like floaters, bob on top of the water. I think I can see the roof of our house. It's hard to tell, there are only the tips of roofs, the very highest point. The rest is under dirty green water. Danielle's duplex would be over there, if it were there. It's not.

There's a note near the bottom of the page: *For those who live in the southern part of Plaquemines Parish: We encourage you to seek employment near your current location. It may be nine months to a year before residents are allowed back into the parish. It is heart-wrenching to see what has happened to the place we call home. You will not recognize your community and at times will find yourself lost and confused.*

My face is burning, my stomach clenched. I start a "new discussion" in the Plaquemines Parish forum. *Looking for Desiree and Danielle Watts* is the subject. *If anyone has information on them, please respond. Last heard from on August 28 from their home in Bayou Perdu.*

When I get back to the room, the mood is solemn, the way it is after there's been a big argument. I can't look anyone in the eye. "Bayou Perdu is completely underwater. They say we can't go back for nine months," I say emotionlessly.

"Does that mean they're not going to do the Orange Queen this year?" Mandy shrieks.

Mama stands up and starts throwing things in a bag. "We're going to Cel's house," she says.

Refugees

AUNT CEL LIVES IN a two-story brick house in a nice neighborhood in Atlanta. It's not super-fancy, but it's way bigger and newer than ours. Walking in is a relief after the hotel. It's a home. There is wall-to-wall carpeting, and everything is really clean and orderly.

"Come on in," says Aunt Cel, hugging each of us. She's still in her work clothes: a blue suit and tan pantyhose and low-heeled shoes. Mama would call them pumps. "Here, let me help you with that." Aunt Cel is tall and no-nonsense. It's not that she's not warm — when she hugs you, it's strong and you feel like she puts her all into it. "Vangie, John — you're in my room. Don't argue, that's how it's going to be. Hi, Mama." She hugs Mamere a minute longer. "Mamere and I will take the guest room. Girls, you've got Ami's old room."

We take our stuff up. There's not much to take. The carpeting on the stairs is plush, off-white. At staggered levels on the wall beside the stairs, there are pictures of Ami through the years: baby pictures, graduation portraits. There's a black-and-white picture of Mamere and Grandpere's wedding, and a sepia-toned one of Mamere and her sisters when they were little in old-fashioned clothes and bare feet on the porch of their bayou shack. There's Mama and Aunt Cel with their feathered haircuts in the '70s. And us — the extended-family picture that Aunt Cel hired a photographer to take two Thanksgivings ago. At the time, it felt so silly — we're all wearing black tops and jeans like we're members of some team. The Beauchamp team. But now I can't describe how it feels to see it. That we're important enough to her to be on her wall. It feels like that little part that Aunt Cel has always occupied in my life — the once-a-year trip for Thanksgiving and for my cousin's graduations — has tripled, quadrupled. We have another home because we have family. It's like a piece of the shipwreck that I found bobbing in the water and I can grab onto it to keep me afloat. It's something Danielle doesn't have.

Not knowing where she is has gone from shocking pain

to a nearly all-consuming thought to a dull ache. There have been times when I thought our friendship was so strong that we had some kind of psychic connection. But no matter how much I will her to call me, she doesn't call.

The room Mandy and I are going to share has a big double bed with lots of pillows. The closet is spacious, but neither of us has anything to put in it anyway. Mandy heads off immediately to take a shower. I take off my shoes and lie down on the cool cotton comforter. It smells like fabric softener. Like someone else's house. I try to remember what our house smelled like. It's there, somewhere in my memory, but I can't reach it. Did it smell like garlic? Fried seafood? Orange blossoms, sometimes? Mandy comes back from the shower with one towel wrapped around her head and the other around her body. She starts going through the dresser drawers.

"What?" she says when she turns to find me giving her a reproachful stare. "Aunt Cel said we could." She picks out an old pair of sweatpants and a sweatshirt with a Georgia Bulldog on it. "Oh, Lord, it's a good thing nobody from home can see me in this."

"You'll never get into LSU now."

Dinner is spaghetti and salad and some bread in a basket—nothing that we would ever have at home. Before I even start eating, I feel suddenly exhausted, like I can barely lift my head. I've gotten through the past five days on adrenaline. Now that I've relaxed a tiny bit, I'm falling apart. I can only manage to make occasional appreciative sounds to show Aunt Cel that I'm enjoying my dinner. Nobody is really talking, just complimenting her on her cooking.

"Oh, please," she says, brushing it off. "Do you know how intimidating it is to cook for the likes of you? Vangie's the one who got all the talent in the family. I can barely boil water."

When dinner's over and Mandy and I have cleared away the dishes, Aunt Cel asks us all to come back to the table. It's a big round one, pushed into an alcove surrounded by built-in benches with cushions. There's a pendant light hanging above it, almost like a spotlight that's shining on her as she starts to speak.

"I know you're all in shock and probably don't want to think about this yet," she starts out. "But it may be a long time before everything gets sorted out. So I'm proposing the following." She looks around and catches everyone at the table in the eye. I can see why she's the boss where she works. She tells us that she's going to enroll us in high school and help Mama and Daddy fill out the FEMA paperwork at the Red Cross. I imagine her as a general. She's mapping out our battle plan. No one disagrees.

"I spoke to Jim," she continues, speaking of her ex-husband, who's a real-estate investor. "He's got a condo that's going to be available next week. You can have it as long as you need it. It's a two-bedroom, so it will be tight, but Mamere can stay here with me. It'll be a chance to make up for a lot of lost time. With all your bookkeeping experience, Vangie, we can find you something at my office. Now, John, Jim knows someone at the marina north of town. I know it's not exactly the same, but you need work and we might be able to help you find some odd jobs."

I finally look up at Daddy. I can't tell what the expression on his face means. "Cel, we're so grateful for everything you're doing for us," he says. There's something in his voice. He's ashamed that he has to be in the position of getting and not giving.

Aunt Cel's voice turns even more serious. "Now, I'm going to say this once and once only. I will not hear any discussion about money or paying for things, and if you bring it up, I will be angry. It is my privilege to be able to help my family when they need it. When everyone's back on their feet again, it's forgotten."

The conversation turns to what has happened to whom. Have we heard from so-and-so? Mrs. Menil? Yes, she's with Delbert. His house uptown was barely scratched. I guess she's finally moved in with him permanently. She's got no choice now. Mr. Ray is in Baton Rouge with his brother's family. On and on. I see my chance to blurt out "Can I use your computer? To check to see if Danielle got my message?"

Aunt Cel looks at me. "Desiree Watts's daughter? Are they missing?"

That awful, overwhelming tension seizes the table.

"They didn't have a car. We're not sure how they got out," says Mamere. "No one has heard from them."

Aunt Cel gives Mama a serious look. "The computer's in the office. Go on ahead," she says to me.

I go straight to my message on the Plaquemines Parish board. Nothing. The New Orleans boards are full of updates, but no one seems to know or care what has happened to Bayou Perdu.

Later, Mandy and I are in the double bed, both wearing Ami's old clothes. It's so dark in here, and there's a quietness that I'm not used to. It's not just that you can't hear what's going on outside; it's that each room has its own quietness.

"Insulation," says Mandy. "And central air conditioning." Two things we've never had.

Despite my earlier exhaustion, I can't go right to sleep. I can feel Mandy awake next to me.

"I can't believe she's making us sign up for school," she says finally.

"I think it's, you know, the law," I say. "We're dropouts right now. Can't be homeless and dropouts."

"You know tomorrow night would have been the ring dance and Sunday, the Orange Queen court selection," Mandy continues. "I really thought I had a chance this year."

It's so unlike her to open up to me, to give me a glimpse into what she's really feeling, to show a chink in her armor.

66

For a moment at least, it's like we're little again, when we used to get along sometimes, play together.

"Who knows what they have up here? Maybe you can be the Peach Queen instead."

A pillow thumps softly but with force into the side of my head. I go to sleep feeling less tense than I have since we left home.

The next morning, Aunt Cel drives us to the school where Ami went. A SCHOOL OF EXCELLENCE, the sign in front proclaims. It's a huge place — it looks like a college. The parking lot is full of cars — nice new ones. The least nice one is close to the kind of car you'd see in the parking lot of Bayou Perdu High School. Inside, the lighting is bright and everything looks so clean and new. We follow Aunt Cel into the front office. The secretary, sitting at a tall counter like the one at the library, looks up and smiles. "Welcome back, Mrs. James," she says. "What can I do for you?"

"These are my nieces from Louisiana," says Aunt Cel. "They're going to be staying with us for a while. I've got the paperwork here from the district office."

The secretary gives us a look as if we have some fatal disease. "Oh. I'm so sorry. We've had some other Katrina refugees come in from Mobile. Let's see, then. A junior and a senior. Do you girls know what you were enrolled in at your old school?"

A hot anger wells up in me. Everyone is using that word now. *Refugees. Yes, we're refugees from southern Louisiana, but we're not stupid. I do happen to remember what classes I was taking.* I pull out my fall schedule and hand it to her.

"Let's see. Evangeline, I've got an opening in an English class that I think will work. For PE, we've got a yoga that would fit with this schedule. Would that be OK?"

Yoga? I nod. I think about how everyone at home would flip out if they knew I was going to a school that offers *yoga.* I'm not entirely sure what it is.

The secretary prints out a schedule and gives us our e-mail log-in and password, then says "Hold on a minute" and comes back with someone who looks like a student, except that her clothes are a little worky.

"I'd like you to meet our school counselor, Ms. Bell," she says.

Ms. Bell shakes hands with us as if we're grown-ups. She seems nice.

"Ms. Bell is available anytime you need to talk, considering what you've been through. I know she's helped some of our other Katrina refugees."

Maybe I'm reading too much into it, but Ms. Bell seems to cringe a little at the use of that word, too. "Strictly confidential. Strictly voluntary," she says. "If you ever find you need to talk to someone, my office is right through that door." She points to the left.

I know I am never going to come talk to this woman.

On the way back home, Aunt Cel brings us to the temporary Katrina shelter the Red Cross has set up at the YMCA
where refugees like us can fill out paperwork for FEMA and
get any updates on federal assistance. It's the fanciest YMCA
you've ever seen. It makes the Y in Bayou Perdu look like
a dump.

When you walk in the door to the gym part, cots are
arranged in rows across the floor. A few people are lying on
them, asleep. Others are lying on their backs reading. Some
people come in and out of what must be the locker rooms.
There's a row of tables set up on the far wall with laptops on
them. The sound of a baby crying echoes through the huge
space. It smells like chlorine. There must be a pool around
here. I wonder if Danielle is in a place like this somewhere.
That wouldn't be so bad. Not like the endless rows of cots at
the Astrodome I've seen on TV.

A friendly-looking woman is sitting at the table inside
the door. "Welcome. Y'all here from the Gulf?" She's smiling.
She reminds me of Kendra's aunt Mechelle. She's the first
person who hasn't made me feel like I'm an object of pity.
"Come on in. Do you have some kind of ID?"

Mandy pulls out her license and hands it to her. "Oh, y'all
from Plaquemines, huh?" She pronounces it right. *Plak-uh-
min.* "I got people in St. Bernard. They're stayin' by my aunt
in Opelousas, but I told 'em they could come up here. Now,
what can I do for you?"

We fill out forms and she tells us we're welcome to

"shop the boutique" at the back of the gym, full of stuff that people have donated, like old sweats and T-shirts from 5K races that they ran or jackets with shoulder pads and floral blouses. I pick up a few solid-color T-shirts.

"Eww," says Mandy, holding up a huge bra. "I can't believe people donate their underwear."

As we're leaving, I approach the shelter lady. "Is there any way you can check to see if someone is staying in another shelter somewhere? I'm looking for a friend."

"You got her number?"

"She doesn't have a cell phone."

"Do you have one?"

I nod.

"Give me her name and I'll see what I can find out for you," she says, smiling. When I slip her the number, she opens a lockbox to put it in and gestures to me to come closer. She presses a two-hundred-dollar Old Navy gift card into my hand. "Now, I don't do this for everybody," she says. "But a girl's got to look nice. Here's one for your sister, too."

I've never had two hundred dollars to spend on clothes in my life. It seems such strange compensation for all we've lost. "Thank you so much, but this is too much. I couldn't take this," I say, embarrassed by her generosity.

The shelter woman smiles with a kind of understanding. "People want to help," she says. "It's OK to let them."

* * *

Uncle Jim's "investment property," which he usually rents out to college students, might sit empty for a while. He says we'll be doing him a favor if we live in it and keep it up. It's a two-bedroom town house at the Village at Pine Ridge Pond. There's a big sign that proclaims its name stuck to the fake stone wall that surrounds the whole complex. The sign—which is made of something plastic pretending to be wood—is coming unglued, and it's sagging in one corner. There are little poster-board signs stuck into the grass in front of the flower beds: FIRST MONTH FREE, FITNESS CLUB, WASHER/DRYER CONNECTIONS, FULLY FURNISHED.

I guess you could call the location a ridge; it's overlooking the expressway with one of those huge concrete-slab walls forming a barrier in between. There are a couple of scraggly pines sticking out of the red clay, some scattered pine needles beneath them. Orange mulch. There is a sad pond with some benches next to it. The two-story, grayish town houses are grouped together with parking spots out front. Since they all look alike, it takes us a while to find ours. The building has a big *C* on the side.

"Here we are," says Mama. "Home sweet home." She turns with a forced cheerful look on her face and meets my eyes, then Mandy's. The tension in the truck is as thick as the air in southern Louisiana in August.

When we get out, I can hear the distinct *whoosh* of the cars passing by on the expressway the same way you can hear the ocean when you're close to the beach. The gray door ahead is ours: 501-C.

Mama turns the key and opens the door into a tiled hallway with a stairway immediately ahead. Off to the side is the living room: gray carpet and one of those sectional sofa sets in gray pleather. There are metal venetian blinds in the window. Mama catches my eyes again. This time, she looks genuinely excited. She gestures to all the furnishings like a model on a game show. "How about this? Can you believe the TV? Saints games are gonna look good on that, huh, John?" Daddy's face is blank.

She glides into the kitchen, which begins beyond the little bar and bar stools at the back of the room, turns, and gasps, "Would you look at this?" It's a galley kitchen with stainless-steel appliances, granite countertops. Mama's face is flush, like a little girl on Christmas morning. She's already opened the fridge. "Side-by-side," she almost squeals. "This whole side is a freezer! Mandy, look!"

"Oh, yeah, lots of space," says Mandy. But I can tell her heart's not really in it, either.

Upstairs, there's a bathroom in the hall and two bedrooms. The room Mandy and I will share has what looks like an old-fashioned little girl's bedroom set. There are twin beds with a nightstand in between. Mama and Daddy's room has its own bathroom.

"This is nice," says Mama. "This'll be just fine."

"I'll go get the stuff from the truck," says Daddy.

"That won't take long," says Mandy. She wanders back into our room and plops down on the edge of the bed. "I wish we could have stayed with Aunt Cel," she says. "This place sucks."

"It's only for a little while. Four months maybe."

Mandy grunts. "You're dreaming. You really think we're going to be back in Bayou Perdu by spring?"

"We're going to have a FEMA trailer," I say. "We'll have a trailer by, like, Mardi Gras."

Mandy throws herself back on the bed. "Right."

I want to rewind to the day before my sixteenth birthday, when my whole life stretched out before me, sparkling like the sun on the clear water of a back-bayou channel. When my life had a rhythm and I knew my place in it.

Mandy and I roll into the parking lot of Brookdale High School for our first day in the car that an elderly man at Aunt Cel's church donated because he lost his mind. It is, if not the uncoolest ride in the parking lot, at least in the top ten. I think I see a Ford Taurus parked way over where no one can see the driver getting out of it. We stop and look at each other for a second before opening the front door of the school.

"I want to go by Amanda up here," Mandy whispers as people sweep past us. "Don't call me Mandy in front of anyone."

"OK, Mandy."

She shoots me the bird and steps inside.

I had been imagining the first day of this new school like one of those bad teen movies: I open the door and everyone turns and stares as I walk down the hall. Some point or whisper behind their hands. But it couldn't be more different. We are invisible. Everyone rushes by to their classes, talks with their friends. I don't think anyone would have known that we were new because there are so many people—how could you know them all?

The lady at the front desk gives us a *map* to our classes. There are different wings, other buildings. I get lost on the way to homeroom and arrive late. No one gives me more than a glance as I walk in. Everyone looks so much older than me. They're way more dressed up than we would ever be for school at home if we didn't wear uniforms. They're in high-heeled boots, tons of accessories, like everyone's going clubbing in the Quarter. I wish Danielle could see this. Wherever she is. If she is somewhere. The bell rings and I try to check the map inconspicuously in the hall so that I can figure out where my next class is.

I find my political science class as the bell rings. I don't have the book. The teacher, a plump lady named Mrs. Economou, tells me to look on with the person next to me, a guy who's wearing the closest thing I've seen to what I'd consider normal clothes: jeans, a long-sleeved plain T-shirt, and tennis shoes. He smiles. Seems nice enough. I try to follow along. After about ten minutes, Mrs. Economou tells us to break up into groups to discuss the three questions she wrote on the board. People groan and mutter and metal scrapes the floor as everyone shifts their desks together. I find myself in a group of four with my book partner, this guy who looks like a big jock, and a serious-looking girl dressed all in black.

I have a hard time keeping up. It's mostly the girl in black talking and the football player responding with wisecracks. The nice guy who shared the book adds the occasional comment, but you can tell he doesn't want to get caught up in the drama between the other two. His name is Tate. The girl's name is Ariel. She's taking all the notes, writing down everything that she herself is saying.

When the bell rings, Tate slides the book to me. "Here. You keep it. My neighbor has one I can borrow if I need it."

"Are you sure? It may be just a few weeks, but it could be longer," I protest.

"I'm sure. My number's written inside the front cover. We can study sometime if you want."

"Thanks." There's something about the way he offers me his number that doesn't seem like a come-on. I'm grateful for that. For a second, I feel almost like a normal person.

"So, Amanda," I joke to Mandy when we get in the car after school. "How was your day?"

She shakes her head. "Whatever. Who cares? You said it. We're only here for a few months."

"That good, huh?"

"It was fine. There was this guy totally checking me out."

And so our new life here continues.

Things that we lost seem to remind us of their absence only when we need them.

Almost every day, Mandy stands in front of that big, near-empty closet and says, "I wish I'd brought that belt," or "Today would be the perfect day for that white shirt." She stares into the blankness like she can make whatever it was come back if she stays there long enough.

Sometimes it's the most unexpected thing, like a whiff of a certain laundry detergent or cleaner, that will bring something or someone back into my mind. The librarian at school wears the same perfume as Miss Helen at the Dollar Store in Bayou Perdu. What happened to Miss Helen? I wonder. Is she living in some shelter in Baton Rouge or Houston? Will I ever see her again? It's not that we were close. She's another part of my life that was swept away, another missing piece. Checking the message boards on the *Times-Picayune* website for some sign from Danielle has become a reflex for me. Whenever I'm in the library at school, I'll log in, knowing I won't find anything. I've even just typed her name into Google to see if anything comes up, but so far I've only found a woman named Danielle Watts who lives in Australia, and about three who live in other places but aren't her. I've called that woman at the YMCA shelter three times, but she hasn't found anything.

When I call Kendra, she says that there's so many kids from New Orleans in Houston schools that there's been a backlash. The Houston gangs are harassing New Orleans kids, and New Orleans kids are forming their own gangs. Someone spray-painted GO HOME on a bunch of the New Orleans kids' lockers, and someone else painted NO right back. No one has messed with Kendra yet. She's big, you know. But there's a group of girls who always talk trash about New Orleans when she walks past. "Too stupid to realize it's a city, not a state," she grumbles. Ms. Denise's job at the navy base is waiting for her when they get operational again. They're going back as soon as they can, Kendra says. She's not going to let this get her off track from her scholarship hopes.

At home, Daddy is planted constantly in front of the TV, watching Hurricane Katrina coverage. Everyone wants someone to blame. It could be Mayor Nagin for not getting all those old folks and poor folks out of the Ninth Ward where they drowned. Or it could be Governor Blanco for not asking for enough help. Or is it FEMA for their slow response? Or the federal government and President Bush for flying over the coast instead of coming down to earth and showing some real concern? Some people think the dumb southern Louisiana and Mississippi people who were too stubborn to leave got what they deserved. What were they thinking living in Hurricane Alley in the first place? What could they expect? When Daddy hears this, he shakes his head. "Everybody knows better," he mutters. "But they like their fresh shrimp, don't they?"

The subject comes up in Political Science. Mrs. Economou is talking about the role of the U.S. government. "What does the government have an obligation to provide for its citizens?" she asks.

One girl raises her hand. "To provide roads, military protection, and Social Security?"

"Public safety," says another girl. "You know, like the justice system."

"OK, that's part of it," says Mrs. Economou. "But one person's safety is another's intrusion into privacy. What are the limits? Who decides? There will always be cases that push the limits and cause us to reexamine what we believe. When something unprecedented happens. Take Hurricane Katrina, for example. We have this perfect example of a conflict, when the role of the government is under discussion. Was the government obliged to get people out of their homes, by force if necessary, in order to save their lives? Was what happened at the Superdome a failure of government? And is the government obliged to rebuild the Gulf Coast when another hurricane could wipe it all out again?"

She turns to me. Here it comes.

"Evangeline," she says, as if she just remembered I was there. "I'd be curious to know what you think."

It's like every eye in the room is on me. I am now the spokesperson for all of Louisiana. For every Katrina refugee.

I want to disappear under the floor. But if I'm going to have to speak for all of us, I'm going to take my time and collect my thoughts. I can almost hear a giant clock ticking in my head.

I start, my voice sounding small. "About making people leave. I think people just don't understand. There are hurricanes every year. It's part of life. More people probably die from traffic accidents here every year than have died in hurricanes in Louisiana in a century." There are a few snickers. "It's not a place that everyone would choose to live, but it's our home."

I am horrified to feel a lump growing in my throat. *Please don't cry. Please don't cry,* I urge myself. I have to think of something else to say. Something smart. But the word *home* has broken me. In a split second, all the weight of that word washes over me like a massive wave and crushes me. If I open my mouth again, I'm going to sob. So I stare at my desk and the awkward silence envelops me.

"All right, then," says Mrs. Economou briskly. "Anyone else?"

I look up in time to see Ariel, who is still in black and still sending out that hostile energy, thrusting her hand into the air. I feel a rush of gratitude toward her for taking the focus away from me.

"Yes, Ariel?"

"I don't understand why it's even a question that we should rebuild the Gulf Coast and New Orleans. I mean, we are willing to go in and blow up and then rebuild two entire foreign countries that most Americans can't find on a map, and we can't get trucks with food and medicine into New Orleans?" Her voice is rising and her face has hardened. She is just getting started. "If the government has any obligation, any purpose, that should be it. To provide for its citizens in the times of greatest need and to bring the power of the collective to bear for the individual."

I look around the classroom. Most people are not listening to her. Those who are look annoyed with her. I'm in awe of her.

Mrs. Economou uses this opportunity to segue back to the book. "Yes, well, that brings us back to page one hundred seventy-five and the framing of the constitution . . ."

I don't know if it's my breakdown that causes him to pity me, but the next day, Tate invites me to go with the Outdoor Adventure Club on a weekend rafting trip up to the mountains in North Georgia. It's just as friends, I'm sure, and it's free. I'm sure Danielle would make a big deal about it and dance around squealing, "He *likes* you!" But I don't feel that way at all. He's just a nice guy. So I go.

"It's beautiful up there — you'll love it," he says, sitting next to me in the van on the way up. I wonder if it's obvious that living in the city is draining the life out of me.

The countryside rolls by, wooded, with the fall colors coming up. Then the land starts to rise, gradually at first. Rushing creeks border the winding roads, the rocky walls of mountains rising up all around. Beautiful, yes, but I feel almost suffocated. For me, the beauty of Bayou Perdu is all that *limitlessness,* the water and sky going on and on forever. A place where you are completely free.

I don't enjoy anything about rafting, bumping along over rapids. Water just isn't supposed to *race.* It flows; it sings; it even roars sometimes. But it's not in a hurry.

After school the next week, I go fishing and canoeing with the club on this man-made lake outside of Atlanta. No one even knows what to do with their rods. They've got all the wrong bait. You can see from one end of the lake to the other. When we get out on the water, no one is really *serious* about fishing. Then again, why would they be? There's no challenge in it here. All I can think is, I may be some Katrina victim, but at least I know what a proper lake is. These people get so excited about paddling around in this little baby pool stocked with fish they've trucked in. I actually feel sorry for them.

I miss the water, the birds, the wind through the marsh grass. I miss the sunset and the sound of that hard, hard rain falling on the roof. I miss the smell of salt in the air, that awful heat rising up from the docks. I feel sore all the time from all the missing. Bruises just beneath the surface. Invisible.

I see the damage in Daddy, too. He gets work as a handyman some days by standing outside in a parking lot with a bunch of mostly Mexican guys and waiting to see if someone will come by and choose him. On the days he works, he comes home, pops a beer, and sits on the couch flipping the channels of that big, big TV. He is lost, as lost as Bayou Perdu.

But Mama. She is different here. She's happier. She likes putting on a skirt and stockings to go to work. She likes wearing heels. She could never have done that at the diner. She likes sitting at a desk and answering the phone. She probably likes going to the break room and making micro-wave popcorn for herself. She's not hot and dirty, and there's no one making demands of her every minute. She doesn't burn her fingers or have to explain that she's run out of the special. Most of all, I thinks she likes that she's not the one making all the decisions — having to fire people or beg for credit from the bank. She shows up, does her job, and leaves. Sometimes on the way home, she stops and goes shopping because she can and buys another pair of shoes or a set of place mats that were on sale. You can tell, she feels like she's really moving up in the world.

Mandy, though, is moving in the opposite direction. She got right to work making sure everyone knew that she was someone important where she came from. But the truth is, she's not going to cut it with the popular crowd here. She may have been the biggest thing at Bayou Perdu High School, but the cheerleaders here are out of her league. She's "country come to town," as Mamere would say. I can see her trying and missing the mark. Since the football cheerleading squad has been in place since last spring, she tries out for basketball cheerleading. On the day the announcement is made, I find her in our bedroom crying hard, mascara running down her face.

I sit down next to her on the bed in the dark. "Sorry," I say without asking what happened. I know.

"It's pathetic," she chokes out. "I can't even make *basketball* cheerleading." She says the word *basketball* like it's chess or something. Like it's the most pitiful thing anyone could ever cheer about.

I've always found her cheerleading obsession shallow and stupid, but I get it. I put my arm around her.

She sobs harder. "I wasn't good enough."

Mamere says that there's always going to be people with more than you and those with less. You can't spend your time looking around for things you don't have. But so much of what Mandy had, what she was, was dependent on having more than others: prettier, more popular, the most boyfriends. Without it, I don't think she knows who she is anymore.

"Mandy." I put my hand under her chin to lift her face so she'll look at me, like a little kid who fell on the playground.

"You're good at everything you do. You always have been. Remember the Mandy on homecoming court every single year? And in the state softball championship? This is a setback. You can get past it."

"No," she says fiercely. "I'm not her anymore. She's gone."

As if to underscore her point, she makes this new friend called Lacy. She's one of those girls who wear way too much makeup and talk with that fake ghetto accent. She's what Mamere would call "common." People always say that when you go to a new school, the good kids already have their friends and the only ones who are looking for more are the bad ones. I'm a little surprised that Mandy would fall for that, but then again, she has an air of desperation around her here and like attracts like, I guess.

I'm not sure what that says about me, though, because I seem to be attracting Tate. I don't know what he could possibly see in me. A girl with a possibly-dead best friend who's dead inside herself. I'm wearing other people's clothes and living in someone else's house. But on the trip to the lake, he seemed taken with the fact that I know how to fish and operate an outboard. He laughs at my jokes as if I'm wildly amusing. I catch him looking and smiling at me during class. It's sweet, I guess. It's something. I wish I could talk about it with Danielle. But I'm still a little surprised when he asks me to the homecoming dance. "I mean, just as friends, of course," he adds hastily in response to the look on my face.

"Never been to one of these things before. Thought it might be good people-watching."

"Sure. Sounds fun," I lie. Sixteen years in Bayou Perdu and no date. Two weeks at Brookdale High and I've got a date to homecoming.

"*You've* got a date to homecoming? Seriously? Now I've heard everything," sneers Mandy, who does *not* have a date to homecoming.

"The world's gone mad," I deadpan to her.

I get ready at Aunt Cel's. Mamere fixes up an old dress of Ami's from the '90s so I can wear it in public. "Oh, so *now* you'll wear a dress," Mandy says, shaking her head.

For the second time in as many months and in our lives, Mandy is trying to get me ready for a moment that should have been hers. "Here," she says, bringing out a little jeweled headband that she must have found in Ami's bedroom. "You need something for your hair. Just come on. No one from home is here to see you."

It looks suspiciously like a crown. Without a shrimp. I roll my eyes. "Fine." I am playing a role. A normal girl going to a homecoming dance. This is what she would wear.

Tate comes to pick me up at Aunt Cel's and has a corsage and everything. He is polite to my family. We get into his nice car. "You look really pretty," he says.

"Thanks," I say.

"What kind of music do you like?" he asks.

"Lots of different kinds. Most kinds. You?"

"Me too, I guess."

Then silence.

"So, do you have brothers or sisters?" Boy, I'm really scraping the bottom of the getting-to-know-you question barrel here, but he's not doing a lot to keep the conversation going.

We get to school and people are stepping out of limos in dresses like you'd see on the red carpet on TV. In fact, there is a red carpet leading into the gym. I feel painfully unsophisticated. No plunging neckline or four-inch heels. No professional makeup job and updo.

This dance is catered. There are waiters in white shirts and black pants walking around with trays of hors d'oeuvres. There's a DJ and a light show. In Bayou Perdu, we would have a band and a crawfish boil under the boatshed. I've felt out of place here before, every minute of every day. But this is like another planet to me. I wish Danielle were here so we could talk about it.

Tate finds his friends, who, to my great relief, also look unsophisticated and out of place. They're not jocks, not stoners. There's nothing obviously academic or high-achieving about them. They're just normal. I make small talk with one of the other girls, Mary Katherine.

"I like your dress," she says.

"Oh, it's from the nineties," I say. Why can't I accept a

compliment? "I like yours, too," I add quickly.

"Thanks!" she says. "Are you and Tate dating?"

"No, just friends. I just moved here. He's being nice."

She nods. "He's like that. So sweet."

Our conversation fades away because it's hard to hear over the throbbing hip-hop. The DJ switches to more clubby dance music, and a few people get up to dance. I'm terrified that Tate will ask me to dance to this, but he doesn't. The minutes feel like hours. They finally play some mainstream country music like we would have had at home. I'm desperate for something, anything to happen. "Do you know how to two-step?" I ask.

He shakes his head.

"Want to learn?"

He shrugs.

We're off to the side of the dance floor. There are groups and couples out there, some who really know how to dance, others just goofing around because they think country music is so uncool it will be funny to try to dance to it. I show him a few steps, and then we join in with the lines. My heartbeat gets going a little. I find myself smiling, laughing a little. I'm almost having fun. When the song's over, we sit back down.

"That was fun," he says. "You're good at that."

"Really, not," I say. But things feel a little more comfortable with him. Maybe this is not so bad. Maybe. Maybe if I give it time.

I excuse myself for the bathroom, then wait in line with

a bunch of girls who have obviously been sneaking in booze or came drunk already. There's a girl in front of me in sky-high heels, and when she exits the bathroom, she trips and goes splat before I can grab her.

"Are you OK?" I rush to her side to help her up. A guy coming out of the men's room gets her other arm. After she's on her feet, she looks at me with annoyance rather than gratitude and then hobbles away, smoothing out her dress. When she moves, I see the guy who was holding up her other side. It takes a second for his face to register, but when it does, my brain pretty much explodes. It's the guy with the boat from Bayou Valse d'Oiseau. It's Tru.

We stare at each other for what feels like forever. And it really is like a teen movie, where our eyes lock and music and noise around us recedes and there is only this intense shock of staring into each other's eyes in disbelief. I'm sure my mouth is hanging open. His definitely is.

"Gumbo Girl. Evangeline," he says in wonderment. "Every time I see you, you're saving someone. And wearing a crown."

Without saying a word, I reach up and rip the stupid headband off my head, my hair falling all around. But I still can't say anything. I can't reconcile everything that's happening. Me. Him. Here. Me. Him. *Here.*

"This is . . . wow," he says. "This is incredible."

"This is incredible," I manage to repeat stupidly. "Do you—? What—?" I can't finish a sentence. "What are you doing here?" I finally get out. "Do you actually go here now? This actual school?"

"This actual school," he says. "For, like, a month. Do you?"

"Yes. Also for, like, a month."

"Bayou Perdu," he says in a way that I take as shell-shocked shorthand for *I heard. It's gone. I'm sorry.*

"Yeah," I say, nodding. "St. Bernard," meaning the exact same thing.

"Yeah," he says.

"Is your family OK? And the Trans?"

"OK, yeah," he says. "Relatively speaking. We lost everything. But, you know, we're still alive, so . . ."

"Yeah, I know." I feel like something passes silently between us.

"How is Kaye?" I blurt out. "She's not here, too, is she?"

He looks confused. "Who?"

"Kaye Pham. From Bayou Perdu. I thought you guys were dating."

"What?" He looks genuinely surprised. "No. What made you think that?"

Relief washes over me. "She was talking about you at school."

"What? No. No." He shakes his head. "She's nice, but my cousin was just trying to set us up. Unsuccessfully. What did she say, exactly?"

"I don't remember, exactly."

"No, we never even went out. My cousin was just trying to set us up because . . . well, it's a long story," he says. "Not a particularly interesting one."

Just talking about someone from home, something familiar, feels so comforting. Even if we are talking about someone I thought he was dating.

"And you?" he asks. "You're here with someone?"

"Just a friend. Sympathy date. For a Katrina victim. You know how it is." If there was a way for me to downplay this date any further, I don't know what it could be.

He laughs. "I doubt very much that it's a sympathy date. But yes, I know how that is. Refugee status."

"Are you? Here with someone?"

He tugs at his T-shirt, which he's wearing over jeans. "I'm the hired help tonight. The music teacher recruited me. I'm helping with the sound setup." He smiles. Laughs that laugh I remember from that hour or so we spent together back in Bird's Waltz Bayou in another lifetime. A laugh that invites you in somehow. "So you go to this actual school?" he asks, as if he's talking to himself out loud. "And we haven't seen each other?"

"Until now," I say.

"Until now," he repeats.

We talk about our schedules. We're never really near the same place at the same time. My lunch is during his music class, and the music teacher is cool. Since the classroom opens to the back of the soccer field, the teacher lets them go out and practice on the hill near it. Some people take their lunches out there, so maybe we could meet there sometime.

"Sorry, I don't have a phone," he says. "You know how it is. Every penny goes toward buying a new boat."

I nod. "I hear ya. If my dad doesn't get some work soon, mine will probably be gone, too."

"I better get back to work now," he says. "You better get back out there. There may be some people who need help on the dance floor."

"There are definitely people out there who need some serious help," I say. "Gumbo Girl to the rescue."

He turns down the hall toward the back entrance to the gym. And I feel like one of those cartoon characters whose eyes turn into hearts and little birds tweet and float around their heads. I open the door to the gym — to the pop music, the heat, and the purple lights — and I can't stop myself from bopping my head along to the stupid dance song, all the way back to the table. I am bursting. All those SAT words that mean *ecstatic. Ebullient. Elated.*

"You must really like this song," says Tate when I get back to the table, beaming and flush for the first time since we got here with this feeling of possibility, of hope.

I just giggle a stupid, Mandy-ish giggle. "This song rocks," I say. "Wanna dance?"

He gets up and dances with me, looking a little awkward and embarrassed. We dance goofily through a few more songs before his friends start to leave.

"Tonight was really fun," he says as he drops me off.

"It was really fun," I say.

"Well, see you at school," he says. To my relief, he doesn't try to kiss me.

"Thanks for everything," I say, and I rocket into the house, tolerating everyone's questions until I can get up to my room to be by myself with my thoughts, with this thing that is only mine. I take it out and hold it for a moment. He is here. Tru is here. He's not with Kaye. I get to see him again. The only thing that could make it better would be sharing this moment with Danielle.

I remember Mandy telling me one time that men like the chase. For them, dating is the same as fishing. It's all about anticipation. Imagining what will happen. You have to make them work for it. I remember thinking it was ironic that my sister, who really doesn't like fishing, was using fishing analogies to describe dating. But that really is the way it is for her. String the bait and reel them in, keep them hooked or throw them back.

This may indeed be solid advice. I probably should wait at least a few days before wandering out to the soccer field during lunch to try to find him. But lunch has been pure torture for me ever since I got here, and I really can't wait to see him again. I take my paper-bag lunch and head around the side of the building toward the back, past the clusters of people with friends, past the sketchy-looking loners who follow me with their eyes, toward the open back door of the music room. When I turn the corner, I see him sitting on a sunny patch of the hill with two other people. My heart seizes up. My feet carry me forward. Getting closer, I can see that he's got his guitar and the guy to the right has a trombone. The guy on the other side has a bright-pink Mohawk. I walk toward Tru and his friend working out a song on a guitar. I approach, take a deep breath, step out of the shade, and stand in front of them. He stands up immediately, looking a little surprised, but also, to my relief, pleased.

"Hey!" I say, as if getting here took absolutely no emotional effort on my part.

"Hey! You came," he says. "And you brought food."

Now, at least, I feel like I did the right thing. It's good to have the lunch as a prop. "Yep," I say. "Muffaletta and some chips."

The guy with the trombone looks up at me. "Girl, I know you ain't say you got a muffaletta in that bag." While he's obviously exaggerating it, his accent gives him away. He's from New Orleans. And while that's a world away from Bayou Perdu, here that distance is nothing. He's my people.

"Evangeline, this is Derek," Tru says, gesturing to the trombone player. "And Chase." The pink-Mohawk guy. Chase has an open laptop instead of an instrument. "Evangeline's another one of us Katrina refugees."

"I'm surrounded," says Chase. "Welcome to my hometown, such as it is." His voice is a lot higher and his disposition is a lot sunnier than I thought they would be based on his hair.

I pull out the sandwich. "We can split it, if you want," I say.

"In that case, you can visit our music class anytime," says Chase.

Tru smiles and gestures for me to sit down. "After you, mam'zelle," he says. I sit.

"You got real olive spread on that muffaletta?" Derek asks suspiciously.

"I make it myself from Mamere's recipe." I break the muffaletta into four pieces and give one to each of them, keeping the smallest part for myself. I'm focused on Tru, but now I really want Derek's approval of my olive spread. I watch both of them eating it. Tru closes his eyes in a rhapsodic expression. "Oh, yeah, this tastes like home," he says.

Derek nods and gives me a thumbs-up. Chase tilts his head and mumbles, "S'good" through bites. I feel glad that I came.

"You people are really into your food, aren't you?" Chase asks when he finishes swallowing.

"Yes, *we people* are," says Tru. "How could we not be?"

"The food's probably the thing I miss the most," says Derek. "Along with the music. The stuff they try to pass off as 'Cajun food' up here. It's a joke."

94

"Zatarain's is in the international section of the grocery store here," I say.

"Zata-what? What is that?" Chase asks.

"It's a Louisiana secret. If we told you, we'd have to kill you," says Tru.

"You don't know what Zatarain's is?" says Derek. "He probably doesn't know what jambalaya is, either."

"Jamba-what?" says Chase.

"Chase, you just don't understand," says Tru in a mock serious tone. "Do you know what it means to miss New Orleans?" Then he gives Derek a quick conspiratorial look.

Derek nods and picks up his trombone.

Tru picks up his guitar and counts off. Then he starts to play and sing "Do You Know What It Means to Miss New Orleans?" imitating Louis Armstrong's voice, singing about the lazy Mississippi and the Spanish moss and the Mardi Gras memories.

At this point, Derek joins in smoothly with a trombone solo so beautiful it sends chills through me. They both do the chorus. I close my eyes as I listen, and on this red-clay hill in Georgia, I feel closer to home than I have since I left.

I know it's not his usual voice, but I can tell that he's confident, that somewhere in there, Tru's real voice is strong and deep.

"I can't compete with that," says Chase when they're done. "Nobody writes songs like that about missing Atlanta.

People write songs more like 'Get Me the Hell Out of This Crapbox.'"

"I'm not familiar with that one," Tru jokes.

"Give me time," says Chase. "I'm working on it."

I walk back with Tru into the classroom toward the end of class. The teacher, Mr. Heller, gives me a kind of confused look, then a you're-not-supposed-to-be-in-this-classroom look before I head out.

"Sorry we really didn't get to talk," says Tru as we get to the door. "Will you come back again?"

"Sure."

"Tomorrow?"

I laugh. I was hoping he'd say that, but I didn't believe he would. "Sure. Any lunch requests?"

"No, I'm bringing you lunch tomorrow," he says.

I go back to class with a big goofy grin on my face. In Political Science, Tate is more relaxed with me, trying to catch my eye, making faces when someone says something stupid. I know he thinks something is starting between us. I don't have the heart to tell him it's not. I don't have to do anything just yet. I'll just ignore it. I'll just continue to be nice. To be his friend.

The next day, Tru brings us each a *banh mi,* a Vietnamese po'boy with pickled carrots and pork on a baguette, the perfect combination of crunchy, spicy, and slightly sour. Derek and Tru mess around on their instruments. They try to get me to sing.

"I can only sing in French," I say. When Grandpere was alive, he used to play music on the porch in the evenings. He taught me so many songs.

"That's OK. I only play guitar in French. What'cha got for me?"

"Do you know 'C'est Si Triste Sans Lui'? It's kind of bluesy, in a Cajun way."

"Kind of bluesy is my favorite kind. Sing a few lines," he says. "So I can get the chords."

The song comes out of me confidently, from so many nights with Grandpere.

Tru picks up the tune easily. "Très bien, mam'zelle, très bien," he says when we finish.

"Everything sounds good in French," I say. "By the way, Kaye Pham said you were going on American Idol. What's up with that?"

Tru's jaw drops. "She said that? Wow. I did do the auditions last year and I got a callback, but I didn't get the golden ticket. I was going to go to Austin to try again, but, well, you know what happened. It was on September fifth."

That's Derek's cue to share his Katrina story. "That's when I was supposed to be starting a new school for kids who are musical geniuses." He's making a joke, but his expression is serious. Then he tells the real story. People in his neighborhood in New Orleans East weren't really leaving. His dad, who is this kind-of-famous trombone player in New Orleans, was planning on staying, but then he got this strange feeling, almost like a premonition. They threw a few things in the car and left. His dad plays a lot of gigs in Atlanta, so they came up to stay with a club owner he knows. They're living with him now. His grandma was in a nursing home, and the nursing home people were supposed to take her to Baton Rouge on a bus, but they didn't get her out in time. She died from the heat when the electricity went out. So maybe they won't ever go back to New Orleans.

Tru's story doesn't come out all at one time. His family had a pretty big shrimping operation with their other cousins, not the Trans. They evacuated to Baton Rouge to an uncle's house because his two older brothers go to LSU. They lost their boat, which was uninsured, so they had to make money fast to get a new one. They came here to live with another uncle who has a business until they can buy another boat. So they are going to go back to St. Bernard. "Could be a while, though," he says. "Are you going back?"

"As soon as we can," I say. "Whenever we get a trailer. They're going to let us go check out the house and get our stuff next week. If there's anything left."

"Wait, did you two know each other from back home?" Derek asks, sounding confused.

Tru gives me this smile that makes my stomach flip. "We've met," he says. "She came to my rescue."

* * *

We keep it up throughout the week. I bring them roast beef po'boys au jus, because you really can't get good seafood here. And so a pattern, a rhythm, is starting to develop.

Whenever we're not talking or eating, he's on that guitar. You can hear him working things out. He doesn't play the same thing over and over again. The chords are like messages, peeks inside him. Sometimes I feel like he is showing them just to me. He shows me he has sadness and fierceness and tenderness. I catch each note in my ear and let it dissolve, and I find that it makes its way down through my chest, my veins, into my heart. Somehow in there it turns into yearning for more, to be closer to whatever part of him holds all that.

It's so hard to see where this is going without having Danielle to analyze it with. I'm so desperate to know if I'm doing the right thing, I might even ask Kendra. But I'm not desperate enough to mention it to Mandy yet.

There's a little voice in the back of my head that says: *Don't get swept away.* I'm going back to Bayou Perdu. He'll be here and then in St. Bernard. But if the last couple of months have taught me anything, it's that there's no such thing as certainty. There's only now.

We finally get word that we can go back. Forty-eight hours to get in, inspect your property, collect what you can salvage, and get out again.

The signs of the storm start when we get to Mobile: trees with broken branches, the breaks still looking fresh. Nothing has had enough time to heal. The road signs are torn down and detour signs are in their place. Exits blocked off. Military checkpoints.

Then the destruction starts coming at me fast. The telephone poles are leaning in toward the road as we approach, as if they want us to come closer so they can tell us what they saw. There's a church in the middle of the road, as though it used all its strength to hoist itself up to beg us to stay. The timing feels off. We shouldn't have gotten to that church yet. It's a good mile up the road from where it should be.

There's an eighteen-wheeler with its back wheels in a tree and the front ones on the ground. A school bus like a crumpled-up soda can. There are cows on top of the levee, alive and dead. The live ones move slowly, grazing under a blue, blue sky.

The storm seems to have been selective: snipped off a roof, but left the body of the house. Curtains flutter in the frame where a window used to be.

"Oh, my God. Oh, my God. Oh, my God," Mandy keeps repeating with each new horror, until Mama snaps, "Will you please shut up!"

But Mandy continues to sob, loudly. She sounds like a wounded animal.

I can't stand it. "Seriously, Mandy, stop it."

Daddy doesn't say anything.

We're coming close to what must be Bayou Perdu now. Where Bayou Perdu used to be. There's Ashley Parker's parents' drugstore. The top of it is still there, but it looks like a huge claw raked across its bottom, pulling off everything down to the metal-beam skeleton. Kendra's house: half the roof and the windows, plus a lot of the siding, are gone. Our Lady of the Sea looks like an inflatable with the air let out. The roof is resting on the foundation, splinters of wood spread all around. There are a few coffins laying here and there, out of place. Like all this was enough to make the dead get up and walk away. Or float away, as the case may be.

Daddy pulls onto Robichaux. Mrs. Menil's house isn't there anymore. There are only concrete steps leading to nowhere. Then there is our home. It looks like a dead fish with its guts hanging out, entrails of rubble and appliances spilling onto the lawn.

"Oh, Jesus," says Mandy.

"Don't take the name of the Lord in vain," Mamere barks. She never barks.

We get out of the truck.

There's an almost indescribable smell of decay in the air. After the smell, the next thing I notice is the silence. The birds haven't come back yet. For a place that was underwater for weeks, it's now bone dry. The ground is powdery dirt.

FEMA has been by: there's a spray-painted symbol on

what's left of the house. A big X with numbers on each side. On the bottom, there's a zero. No victims.

"Nobody goes in but me," says Daddy. "It's not safe." He goes to the truck to retrieve a crate for our salvage.

We stand at a distance observing our home, as if we're having an awkward introduction with a stranger. Daddy goes into the house. Mama starts picking around in the yard, pulling up boards and looking under them. She sticks a few things in her pocket.

Mamere walks around the side to look at the orange grove, and I go with her. There it is, Grandpere's dream, dead, brown, and shriveled from standing under salt water for weeks. I grab onto Mamere's hand and squeeze it. She nods and says nothing. I see a glint of metal from somewhere back in the grove, and I drop Mamere's hand and run to it. It's our pirogue, the little fishing boat, wedged between two trees. I try to push it free. It's really jammed in there. Soon I'm pushing so hard, I'm grunting and sweating, but I've got the back end free and the front loosens up. It falls to the ground. I sit down in it. Mamere comes through the grove to join me. I help her over the side and into the boat. We are sitting in a boat in a dead orange grove.

"Want to go fishing?" she asks. A twinkle comes back into her eye.

"More than anything," I answer.

When we get back to the front of the house, there's a

wild look on Mandy's face, like nothing I've ever seen before. A mix of pain, fury, and disbelief.

"No!" she screams. The next thing I know, she is on the ground, pounding it with her fist. "No. No. NO. NO." She screams again at the top of her lungs, the type of scream that you can't ever get out of your head. She is doubled over, sobs mixed with screams. Nobody moves a muscle until Mamere goes over, kneels down, and puts her arm around her shoulder.

"It's just things, *cherie*," says Mamere, almost cooing, like she would talk to a baby. "It's just things. We're here together. We're all right. We're all right."

I go over and put my arm around Mandy and can feel her body shaking. I am as calm as the eye of that storm. I'm floating above all of this. She calms down a little. We help her up, and Mama walks over and hugs her. Mandy starts sobbing all over again.

Daddy comes out of the house with the crate. There are five things in it: the wooden box of Mamere's silver flatware that she got for her wedding, Mama's favorite copper pot, his waders, my rubber fishing boots, and Mandy's mold-covered softball glove.

"That's it?" says Mama.

He shrugs.

"Any pictures?" she asks.

"They're all water damaged."

"Even so."

He puts down the box and places the items on the ground, then hands her the empty box. "If you want to go look . . ."

She shakes her head.

It takes about two minutes to drive to the diner. To where the diner should have been. All that's left is a pile of rubble, not a single wall standing. All the booths, the appliances, must have floated away. It's so hard to believe that for a few minutes, I think we must be in the wrong place. But there are the usual landmarks. Mr. Ray's gas station is right there, stripped down to the bones. The collapsed post office. The gutted library. I can feel Mama stiffen all the way from the backseat. She gets out of the truck so quickly that by the time I get out, she's already right in the middle of the rubble. I glance quickly at Mamere, whose face is tight with pain.

From beside the truck, I watch Daddy race over to Mama. He puts his arms around her like he's picking up a child who fell off her bike. She pushes him away. She walks around the edges of the rubble, wearing her anger like a suit. She picks up a cement block and uses all her effort to throw it back into the center of the pile.

I help Mamere cross the field of debris to reach Mama. Looking down, I see a laminated menu lying on the ground. I pick it up. Mandy comes up on the other side of Mamere and holds on to her arm.

Mama and Daddy are on the far side of the rubble, but

I can hear her shouts. "Twenty years!" she screams. She picks up whatever's lying there—an empty ten-gallon bottle of cooking oil, a napkin dispenser—and hurls it back into the pile. "Twenty years, twenty years," she repeats over and over.

"All those things you wanted to change. New booths, a better stove. You can make it the way you want it now. You can make it the way you always wanted," Daddy says.

"I can't. I can't start all over. I can't. I don't WANT to start all over. I am NOT starting all over again!" she shrieks. She picks up a tray and hurls it across the debris.

"When everything is rebuilt . . ." Daddy keeps trying. "It's an opportunity. The construction workers need to eat, too. You could hire someone."

Mama's face is almost unrecognizable with rage. "You don't understand. I'm NEVER coming back here."

I feel like someone has dropped an anchor on my chest. She can't mean that. This is our life. She can't turn her back on this place. This place is us. We can be OK. We've got the fight in us.

I look at Mamere for reassurance. But her face is drawn and so old.

Mandy and I exchange the same look. *She didn't mean that, right?*

No one speaks as we go back to the truck. I notice that Mama isn't carrying anything from Vangie's Diner. I have a single laminated menu rolled up in my pocket.

A horse walks slowly down the middle of the road as we drive back to Bayou Perdu.

There's a huge tent in front of where the fire department used to be. A food buffet and rows of tables are set up under it, and around fifty people are clustered inside. The mood is upbeat. You could almost imagine that you're at a crawfish boil. All that's missing is live music.

Sheriff Guidry comes over and shakes Daddy's hand, then pulls him in for a big hug. "Good to see you back, John. Been over to the house yet?"

Daddy nods. "Our pirogue is still there. Wondering if I can bring it over to you and you'll keep an eye on it till we get back?"

Sheriff Guidry nods. He turns his attention to Mama. "Been over to the diner?"

Mama nods stiffly.

"Have you heard from Desiree and Danielle yet?" I shove my way into the conversation.

He shakes his head. "We didn't find them in our airboat rescues, but every home has been searched. They must have gotten out on their own."

He hands me a brochure with a bunch of numbers to call for information about missing people and pats me on the back. "They'll turn up," he says. "People from this community are scattered all over now. Got some in Tennessee. Texas. A lot probably never coming back." He shakes his head and I see my parents exchange a painfully tense look.

Then Sheriff Guidry gets back to his old self. "We could sure use your cookin' around here now, Vangie." He sighs, pointing to the food line. "National Guard was here with the MREs at first. Not as bad as you would think. Then this group came in from a church in Minnesota. Great folks. Just great people." He leans in closer and lowers his voice. "But they don't know a damn thing about cookin'. They tried to make boudin last week." He puts his finger in his mouth as if to gag. "You'll need an escort to get down to the marina. The road's blocked — guess you heard about that. I can take you down in the morning. Meet me back here around nine. You know Bechtel got his boat out already. He said the reds are unbelievable!"

That's a Louisiana fisherman for you. Never let a little thing like the worst natural disaster in history stop you from a good run of reds.

On the way over to sit at one of the tables, I see April Dubcheck, this girl in my grade who I've never really liked. She's boring and prissy and has a really bad accent when she tries to speak French in class. It annoys me to no end. But today she hugs me tight, like I'm her long-lost best friend. She recounts everything she knows about everyone. Trey Halbert, this junior guy, was one of those people the sheriff's office rescued from the choir loft. His family had to hack their way out of their attic. Some of the oystermen stayed on their boats and it's a miracle they're alive. She heard that Amber was in Baton Rouge and Taylor was in Houston. I can't help but feel a little bit spitefully pleased.

April, Mandy, and I all walk over together to Bayou Perdu High. From a distance, you wouldn't really know that anything is too wrong with it. The walls and the ceiling are still standing. But when you get closer, it looks like it's been abandoned for decades. You wouldn't believe that just over a month ago, it was full of students about to start a new year. Most of the windows are blown out, and there's police tape up around the whole building. We duck under it and enter through the gym.

The water must have covered the gym floor for weeks—it's all buckled up, planks of wood rising and falling like waves. I think about Mr. Jerome, the janitor, the hours he spent polishing that floor so it would shine bright enough to see your own reflection. I think about the cheers and clapping, the feet pounding on the bleachers. Me and Danielle sitting up there together. Kendra playing on that court. In another lifetime.

"Hello!" Mandy shouts at the top of her lungs. "Huh. No echo."

April crinkles up her nose. "This is creepy," she whines. "Let's get out of here."

We move into the hall. There are no more ceilings—all those ugly white ceiling tiles have fallen down and the wires are sticking out. Big pink balls of insulation litter the hallway like industrial tumbleweeds. The lockers are rusted and the floor tiles pulled up. There were times, especially freshman year, when I cursed this school and wished it would explode, disappear. Be careful what you wish for.

Someone has cleared all the tables and chairs out of the cafeteria—or maybe that someone was Katrina. In the hall outside it, all the paint has peeled off the walls, but that big engraved sign with the lists of our state championship teams through the years looks untouched.

We walk back to the football stadium. It's still standing, of course. If there's one thing in Bayou Perdu that could withstand anything, it's the football stadium. A military helicopter hovers overhead nearby.

Mandy wanders off onto the track. I'm a good ways behind her, so I can't see her face, but I can feel her sadness from here, just from the way she's holding her head. She scans the field from one end to the other, and then she turns back toward me. She does a cartwheel. Then another.

"Clap your hands!" she commands the empty stadium, then claps her own three times. "Stomp your feet!" She pounds the ground.

I find myself doing what she says.

"Clap your hands! Stomp your feet! Cavaliers that can't be beat! Goooo, Cavs!" She ends with a spread-eagle jump. Her face looks exhilarated, defiant. She's happy to be alive, happier than I've seen her in weeks. She's just getting warmed up. "Who rocks the house? I said the Cavs rock the house, and when the Cavs rock the house, they rock it all the way down!" She's shaking her hips, pivoting around, reliving all those Friday nights.

April Dubcheck looks at her like she's totally lost it.

When she's done, I go over and hug her. My weird, wonderful sister.

"I heard they might not reopen Bayou Perdu High. Not even next year," says April. The words hang in the air. "Everyone's going to have to go to Bellvoir."

Mandy glares at her.

"My mom said we're not coming back here." Why did I say that? Out loud. To April Dubcheck. Who I don't even like.

April crinkles her nose again. "What?" Her tone is one of disbelief.

"My mom says we're not coming back here. Even when we can."

Her eyes widen. "We're coming back even if we have to live in a van. The Dubchecks have been here for four generations. My dad says it would take more than a hurricane to keep us out of here."

There is no one in the world I hate more than April Dubcheck right now. That should be us. *We're* the resilient ones.

When we get back to the tent, dinner is starting. The Minnesotans have attempted to make po'boys. They are such nice folks, no one wants to tell them that you can't give Louisianans a po'boy without asking if they want it dressed. It's on bread that looks like a hamburger roll. When I turn to Mamere, who's behind me in line, she looks down at her pitiful sandwich and raises her eyebrows. "Bless their hearts," she mutters. Several people come up and make versions of the same joke to Mamere and Mama. "We need you ladies here real bad. Forget the hurricane. We're going to starve to death!" Ashley Parker's dad bangs on the table down from us, pretending to incite a riot. "Food fight! Food fight! We want Vangie's! We want Vangie's!" The other men think this is hilarious.

After dinner, the mood becomes more serious. Heads are huddled together; people speaking in hushed tones. I can hear them talking about their sense of loss, but also their anger. How could the levees have failed? Why weren't officials prepared? Why couldn't the government have done more, acted more quickly to arrive with relief?

You can hear sniffling and crying from different areas of the tent. Mama and Mamere are deep in conversation with a group of ladies. Daddy is with the men. One of the Bayou Perdu High football players who graduated last year is chatting up Mandy, who is clearly enjoying it. I think about *Evangeline*, how the Acadians were in "exile without end . . . on separate coasts . . . scattered like flakes of snow." Just like we are now.

I step outside, past the light that is spilling from the tent, into the dark, far enough away that the sounds of talking fade and I can hear a few crickets, somewhere out there in the marshes. I look up at the sky. The stars are sharp and clear here, so many more than you can see in the city. Everything under it has fallen apart, but the Bayou Perdu sky is the same.

I start walking down the road—the washed-out asphalt that was the road—to Danielle's house. I don't expect to find much, and I don't—a pile of rubble. No walls standing whatsoever. I kick the debris with my foot, trying to sift through it to find some trace of Danielle. But there's nothing I recognize as part of my friend. Just a haunted feeling that enters me. The ghost of our friendship, once so solid, now just a memory, unsubstantial, slipping through my fingers. My throat closes. I take out my phone and dial Kendra as I'm walking back toward the light of the tent in the distance.

"You sound terrible," she says after I say hello.

"I'm in Bayou Perdu."

"How bad is it? Scale of one to ten?"

"I think you'd have to use a number beyond ten."

"Did you see my house?"

"I took some pictures. I'll send them to you. Your house is actually better than most."

"Of course it is," she says, sounding like her usual confident self.

I explain to her about school. The state of the basketball court is distressing to her.

"What about the diner?"

"It's completely gone. Mama says we're not coming back here."

Kendra is silent for a second. "She doesn't mean that," she says. "She's just upset."

"She sounded really convincing."

"Just give her some time. She'll miss the water and the fishing and all."

"That's me, not her."

"Well, she'll miss the crawfish boils, then."

"There's not going to be any crawfish boils here for a while," I say. How do I tell her how empty, how not like our home, it feels? "I went by Danielle's house."

"Any word yet?"

"Nobody has heard anything from them."

"She's probably here in Houston. She probably goes to my high school. It's so big, you'd never know."

"Will you ask around? Or ask your mom if she can?"

"I'm on it."

I smile. Good old Kendra. Solid and real, even on the end of a telephone line. "I miss you," I blurt out.

"Don't get all mushy on me," she says.

A Kiss to Build a Dream On

THE RAIN IS BLOWING in sheets outside the back of the music room, pattering lightly, rhythmically, on the awning that hangs overhead. Tru is harmonizing with it as he searches out a melody. I am listening to the birth of a song.

It opens slowly, the way the petals of an orange blossom take their time to unfurl. It is light dancing on the water, or the wind rustling through the marsh grass. It's sweet and a little sad, but also hopeful. It carries me halfway around the world, to a river whose name I don't know, where waves lap the sides of boats with unfamiliar shapes and the air is scented with exotic flowers.

"Does it have words?" I say. The spell breaks.

He shakes his head. "It's really just stealing riffs from this traditional Vietnamese song," he says. He plays a few chords. Like the ones he just played but more measured. "Like this one. It's kind of hard to translate," he says as he plays on. "Something about the moonlight and clouds. Waiting for someone. It starts raining—it's always raining in Vietnamese songs. Also, there's something in there about soup."

The weather is lousy, so there's no one else outside the music room but us—a rare occasion. I feel like I have kind of, sort of made friends with Derek and Chase in the past couple of weeks. But moments like this, alone with Tru, have become what I wait for, long for. His music has started to trickle into that big empty space in me where home was, where certainty was. He's doing the rescuing this time.

It feels the way it does when I'm fishing before first light with Daddy. When the sun comes up over the water and all those shadows fill into shapes and become clearer. That's the way it is with getting to know him. The colors and shapes fill in slowly. The music, of course, is the first thing that comes into focus. He makes me three CDs of the blues and Dixieland greats he loves: *Tru Tunes,* he labels them, volumes 1, 2, and 3.

"You seem sort of upbeat for someone who's so into the blues," I say.

He tells me about his adopted grandpa and next-door neighbor back in St. Bernard, Mr. Monks. He gave Tru his first guitar and taught him how to play. He was a blues great, Tru says, playing in honky-tonks all around the South in the '40s and '50s. "And you know, it's kind of a misnomer," he says. "The blues aren't really about being sad. Some blues songs are really joyful. It's just a particular type of musical expression." I had never even heard the word *misnomer* before and didn't know what it meant. Tru is smart.

He strums a sitting-on-the-front-porch-in-the-heat-staring-out-at-the-cotton-fields-nursing-a-black-eye-a-hangover-and-a-broken-heart kind of song for me. It makes me ache for home. That muggy, muggy southern Louisiana heat that no one in her right mind would miss. I love that he can make me feel that with his music.

I find out that his family is living in a place like the one we're in, except that it's two families — nine people — in the same amount of space. "It's cozy," he says. But in a way, he says, it's not that weird for them. His parents grew up in refugee camps in Cambodia during the Vietnam War, so they were used to sharing everything. When they bought their trawler, a bunch of cousins chipped in and owned it together. They are used to having lots of people around.

One day, we're walking around the side of the school past those sketchy loners. Tru waves to one of the guys, who's all tatted up and looks like a biker. He goes over, shakes his hand. They laugh a little and he comes back.

"You know that guy?" I ask, not able to hide my surprise.

"Yeah, Sam. He lives in my apartment complex. He's a good guy. He's been through a lot. He's trying to get it together. Addiction is really tough."

Pretty much any other guy I know would have called Sam a dirtbag-loser-crackhead and made jokes about him. Tru has a big heart. It's like there's room in there for everyone.

Conversations with him are not what they are with other people. He cuts to the chase, to the heart of things. "Do you believe in fate?" he asks one day. I don't think anyone has ever asked me that question before.

"I don't think I can anymore. I mean, I used to kind of think there was this great big good thing out there that was supposed to happen to you. That was your fate. And you get it because you deserve it. And now. With everything that's happened. I don't want to think that this was my fate. To lose everything, you know? That I deserved what happened."

"But what if the good thing is wrapped in a bad thing?" he asks, looking serious and thoughtful. "What if when you go through the bad thing, the good thing's on the other end? Or if you respond to the bad thing in the right way, you get the good thing?"

My first thought is that I wonder—I hope—that he is thinking the same thing I am. That maybe we had to go through losing everything to meet each other again. And that's the good thing. "Maybe. Maybe things aren't supposed to be easy. Maybe we're supposed to work for it," I say. "Why, do you believe in fate?"

"My parents really believe in fate. It's a Vietnamese thing. Everybody's name is in a big book with their whole life story written next to it. But I guess they also believe it's written in pencil, because they think you can erase it and rewrite your story if you work hard enough. I think it's an excuse parents give their kids to make them work harder."

"So what's written next to your name?" I ask.

"'Legendary bluesman,' of course," he jokes. He gestures like he's putting his name up in lights. "What do you think yours says?"

I look out into the bland blankness of that soccer field. When I look into my future, what I wish for isn't a job or a title or anything like that. I'm not like Mandy, who wants everyone to admire and love her. For me, it would be enough to have one person. Someone who looks into my eyes and really sees me. To have that, that one person and this whole big ocean to explore and take care of, to keep for those who come after me. That would be enough for me. That would be everything for me. But that, of course, isn't what I say. "I honestly don't know" is what I say.

"What do you love?" he asks, and the *question* makes me blush. "Not love to *do*, but what do you love."

I think back to the times when I've been happiest, when I feel like everything is right with the world. I take a deep breath. "I love water. Open water. The light on it, especially

118

in the late afternoon. I love fishing. Not just catching, but fishing. Waiting and then excitement when you feel a tug on your line. I love birds. All kinds of birds, but especially sea birds. Their feathers and wings and grace. I love the way the seasons come and go, and at home at least, you can actually feel them coming and going. I love music. The way it can take you places you've never been before and how sometimes it just captures exactly what you're feeling. I love Louisiana food. Food that brings people together, I guess. I love belonging to something. Being part of something bigger than myself." I feel embarrassed now. Like I've gone on too long and said too much.

"I am soooo glad you didn't say shopping," he says, half laughing. "I think the things we love are what lead us to our fate, you know? Maybe that's what fate is. When you catch up to the things you love."

There are some people that when you spend time with them, you walk away feeling empty and drained. When I am with him, I walk away feeling so full, overflowing. Better than I was before. I know more, I feel more, my brain and my blood are buzzing. And I need that so much right now.

The shock and pain of missing Danielle, knowing nothing about where she could be, has started to dull a little. I'm still checking the message boards every week. But not every day. I feel guilty for being happy when I'm with Tru, like being happy is a betrayal of her, of her memory. That makes it sound like she's dead. And there's a real chance that she could be. I've gone over and over it in my head. If she is out there, she wouldn't be able to find me, either. I'm not where I'm supposed to be. Maybe she's trying. Maybe she's worried about me, too.

We've gotten in the habit of going to Aunt Cel's every Monday night for red beans and rice. One day after we eat, Aunt Cel and I are alone in her kitchen and she brings up Danielle. "You know," she says hesitantly. "I've been doing some inquiries about your friend. I haven't heard anything concrete yet, but I did get the contact information for someone at the Red Cross who could be very helpful."

Mama walks in. "Did I interrupt something?" she asks.

Aunt Cel looks uncomfortable. "I was just telling Evangeline that I'll do everything I can to help Danielle," she said.

Mama gives Aunt Cel a cold look. "Of course you will," she says. "You're always here to take care of things we can't handle ourselves."

"That's not what I meant," says Aunt Cel. This conversation is suddenly not about me or finding Danielle.

"I sincerely hope that they have started a new life happily somewhere," says Mama, exiting the kitchen on the other side. "But not being a part of it may be the best thing for Evangeline."

I feel a surge of anger boiling up. "Why does she hate Desiree so much?" I spit out at Aunt Cel. "I mean aside from the obvious reasons of her being a terrible mother and wrecking Danielle's life. Which is not Danielle's fault."

"Things happened," Aunt Cel mutters. "It's a long story. Regardless, you're right. It's not Danielle's fault. And I know you won't be satisfied until you know what happened to her. I'm going to keep trying, too. We'll find her."

Mandy. She is lost in a different way. The cheerleading thing sent her into a downward spiral. One day, I saw her as I was coming back from the soccer-field hill. Just as I was crossing that bit of parking lot in front of it, I saw Mandy in the passenger seat of Lacy's car. They both stared out at me. I made a motion for her to roll down the window. Shockingly, she did it.

"What are you doing?" I demanded.

"We're going out to lunch. Pretend you didn't see me."

"You're going to get caught."

"I'm not going to get caught. Don't be such a goody-goody."

Lacy smirked at me and waved. "Laaater," she bleated. Then she squealed out of the parking lot.

Of course they got caught, and of course Mandy got suspended.

Then there is more drama.

Byron has really moved on. There's some girl called Elena in Nashville where he's living now. Mandy broke her own rule and called him after she didn't hear from him for a few weeks. I overheard the whole thing, listened to her trying to act cool on the phone and then descending into desperation. "What's her name? Just tell me, what's her name? Is she a cheerleader? . . . Then what does she do? . . . Great. That's just great. Have a nice life, Byron." I nearly got hit by the phone as she threw it across our bedroom. So I spend a lot of time trying to be where she is not.

The same goes for Mama. But if I'm in the living room, I can hear her on the phone in the kitchen talking to her new work friends. She doesn't sound like herself at all, not just her voice, but her words. She has this attitude that I've never seen before, complaining about the kids and the laundry, talking about going out for margaritas with the gals after work. I don't think she's ever had a margarita. Where would you get a margarita in Bayou Perdu? She's a chameleon. A phony. When she acts like that, I can't look at her.

But it's worse between her and Daddy. If the distance between their feelings about going back to Bayou Perdu was a channel, it's now a gulf. I can hear them arguing through the walls and the closed doors. Not the actual words, just the rhythm of the fight, like the hum of some horrible machine. I don't want to know what they're saying, but it's like slowing down to look at a car wreck. Sometimes I sneak into the hall and stand outside the door to listen.

"We could live in Bellvoir," says Daddy. "I can commute to the marina."

"I don't want to live in Bellvoir. What's in Bellvoir? How are we gonna afford that?"

"There's a trailer park there. We can get a trailer and stay there until we can rebuild."

"Why would I live in a trailer when we've got this nice place here?"

"Here." Daddy's voice steels up. "In a cardboard box in a parking lot. The whole city is a parking lot."

"So you're gonna drive two hours a day and spend all that money on gas to live in a trailer. You think that's better?"

I hate her.

"It's better because that's where our life is," Daddy replies.

"My sister and my mother are here. I've got a good job. Our life can be here now. We don't have to make it harder than it has to be."

"*This* is harder for me, Vangie. There's nothing for me to do here. I am a fisherman, and I'm five hundred miles from the sea. I've never done anything else. I don't know how to do anything else."

"You're not trying, John. You're not trying. You could get a real job. One that's not dependent on the weather and the price of gas and the damn hurricanes. Five years from now, there may not be a fishing industry in Louisiana. We're hardly making do as it is. This is our chance to secure our future. This is it!"

These arguments always end with her making some huge declaration like that and him going silent. These days, I've stopped being sick about them. They're the new normal. Part of the new rhythm in my life, which goes like this: Go to school and count the minutes until lunch. Collect my moments of hope and happiness at lunch with Tru. Sit uncomfortably through Political Science, with Tate there next to me, knowing that I'm eventually going to let him down. Ride home with increasingly hostile and negative Mandy. Tiptoe around Daddy, wondering when the paperwork for our trailer will come, when our ticket home arrives. Wonder when and if I'll ever hear from Danielle. Have a hollow exchange with Mama when she comes home. Play the blues from my *Tru Tunes* CD until Mandy screams at me and makes me turn off. My only breaks come on the two nights a week when I babysit for Aunt Cel's neighbor while she works late, and I blessedly get to sleep over there and take the bus to school in the morning. That's the new rhythm. If my life were a song, it would be almost unlistenable.

But those sweet notes. When they come, they just resonate, like the twang of a single guitar string, vibrating long after it's plucked. While Mandy's suspended, I have to take the bus. After school, I'm walking to catch it when a big, shiny black SUV pulls up alongside me and the window opens. "Hey, lady, want a ride?" It's Chase, and Derek is in the passenger seat. Tru pops his head forward from the backseat.

"Sure," I say, and the back door opens.

I slide in next to Tru. I feel somehow like we've reached a new level. We've gone beyond the bounds of the music room. "Hey," he says. "Welcome to the Chasemobile."

The seats are leather. Everything about this car oozes money. "This is not what I expected you to drive," I say, immediately wishing I'd kept that thought inside.

"I know," says Chase. "It's embarrassing. It totally clashes with my punk image. It's pretty ironic, though, so I'm going with that. By the way, you don't really need to be somewhere, do you?"

I think about it. Home. Homework. Room. Nothing. "Not really."

"Great, you're coming to my house to help us rehearse, then," he says.

I glance over at Tru, who shrugs. "This is why your parents always warn you not to get into the car with strange men," he says.

I feel a pang of guilt. What if Daddy wonders where I am? But he probably won't notice; he notices so little these days.

We pass the main road with all the commercial buildings and apartments, into the nice neighborhoods with tree-lined streets. The houses become bigger. Bigger than Aunt Cel's, even. Chase turns onto a cul-de-sac and up a driveway so long you can't even see the house at the end of it. When we finally arrive, I'm overwhelmed. His house is like one of those country estates in movies. Derek turns around from the front seat and catches the shocked expression I'm trying to conceal. "I know, right?" he says.

"Me and Derek were the first Asian and black guys to come in the door who weren't delivering pizza," says Tru.

"Hey, we're *rich,* not racist," says Chase, getting out and shutting the door. "Yes, I'm loaded. My *parents* are loaded, that is. And I'm an anticapitalist. What can I say? 'I am large, I contain multitudes.' That's Walt Whitman, by the way. I like to sprinkle my conversation with literary quotes just to confuse people who probably think there's no brain under this Mohawk." That's the thing about Chase. He points out the pretentious aspects of his personality before anyone else can. It makes him seem humble. At least to us. Everyone else at school definitely thinks he's pretentious.

The house is enormous inside. Everything you see on home shows on TV—towering ceilings, a big stone fireplace, a grand piano. There doesn't seem to be anybody there. We follow Chase into the kitchen. The pantry is the size of our whole kitchen, stuffed with five of everything. "What are you in the mood for?" he asks. "As you can see, we've got enough to sustain us for a year when the apocalypse comes." He gets out bags of chips and busts them open. The boys get something to drink and I wander into the living room. The shelves are stuffed with books and expensive-looking objects. There's a whole wall of pictures of Chase when he was little: Chase at the piano playing in some important-looking recital; Chase on a boat in someplace that might be

Europe; a bigger Chase in a bigger, fancier recital. From all this I gather he's an only child. He comes up behind me, eating chips. "Oh, so you found my shrine, I see," he says.

"Where were you in these pictures?" I ask, gesturing to his piano recitals.

"That was at Carnegie Hall." He points to the big one. "That other one was at my school," he says.

"How . . . ?" I start.

"Child genius," he says. "The second-youngest person ever accepted to the Manhattan Music Academy. Blah, blah, blah."

I'm dumbfounded. "And now?"

"Got kicked out," he says. "Not serious enough. So it's back home."

Tru comes up behind him. "Yep, and now he's slumming with us." He pats him on the back.

I look at the photos again. "You're a natural blond," I say.

"Yeah, but I think pink suits me better," he says. "It's got the element of surprise."

We go up the massive staircase to his room, which is really a series of rooms, with its own bathroom and a music room. It's bigger than our whole apartment. There's typical guy stuff in here—game console in front of a big flat-screen TV, clothes on the floor—but there's also a shelf full of trophies and ribbons, from his music. There's an electronic keyboard, a guitar, a set of drums, huge speakers, and what looks like a sound-mixing board.

The guys mess around on the instruments. "We better get started if we're going to be ready in two weeks," says Tru.

"Ready for what?"

"Heller works at this 'performance venue' at night, and he said if we came up with an original tune and played it there, we'd get an A," says Derek. "So now we just have to work on a song."

I watch them trying to mix their instruments, trying to blend their musical styles. Tru is working on the drums, Chase on the keyboard, and Derek on his trombone. "Wait, what am I supposed to do?" I ask.

"You can be our manager," says Tru.

"Or our groupie," says Derek. "I always wanted a groupie."

"I'll get T-shirts made with the band name," I say. "As soon as we figure out what that is."

The time passes quickly. I'm watching them zigzag all over the musical map, from modern jazz to R&B. There's a kind of vibe developing. Not a Tru-and-Evangeline-like-each-other vibe, but an Evangeline-is-just-one-of-the-guys vibe. Like at the marina. I'm with him, and that's better than nothing, but my spirits start to sink. Every once in a while I chime in with what I hope are witty comments like "Needs more cowbell" or "Sound pitchy." I'm not even aware of the time until I look out the window and it's dark. I realize I don't have an exit plan. When there is a lull, I say, "Well, I guess I need to head out."

Chase looks up. "Oh, right. You'll be needing a ride."

"I'd better go, too," says Tru.

"Not me," says Derek. "I'm moving in."

As we're coming down the stairs, Chase's mom enters through the front door. You can just tell she is rich. She's probably about my mom's age, but she looks older in a way. She says hello to Tru and Derek, then shakes my hand when Chase introduces me. "Nice to meet you, Evangeline," she says. "I'm Carol Lowndes." She says it the way she'd say it to a grown-up.

When we get in the car, I give Chase directions to Aunt Cel's house because I don't want him to see where we live. Tru sits in the backseat with me again, and when Chase goes around a turn too quickly, Tru slides into me. We sit like that for the rest of the ride, staring ahead, our shoulders, part of our arms, hips, and thighs touching. One time, I look at him and he is looking at me. He doesn't look away. We hold each other's gaze for a few moments. I stay very still, as if moving would make this moment disappear. Does he feel the same way? Is his heart beating as quickly as mine?

At Aunt Cel's, I call home to ask if I can spend the night. Daddy doesn't even seem to have noticed that I was gone. But Aunt Cel has some good news for me. "My contact at the Red Cross found a Watts, family of two, who had been registered at a shelter in Baton Rouge. The whole shelter was cleared out within the first month, though, and the people there were transferred to different places all around the country. He's going to see if he can find out if it was them and where they were transferred to."

I'm afraid to get my hopes up, but I feel a surge of optimism. And I get to spend time with Mamere. I'm brushing her hair, our ritual that makes me feel closer than I feel to anyone.

"How's that young man you went to the dance with?" she asks. "He seemed real nice."

"He is nice," I say. "He's very nice. But it's not that way. There is someone else, though."

"I knew it," says Mamere. "I can tell, the way you've been humming and looking in the mirror more."

I'm mortified. "I have? Really?"

"Mmm-hmm."

I tell her almost the whole story. How I met Tru at the Blessing and then we saw each other again and it seemed like it meant something. Not just because our paths crossed again, but because it happened just when I needed it. How he reminds me of home, but it's more than that. That I've never met anyone like him. I tell her all the things I've noticed about him: his kindness, his humor, his passion for his music.

"Dawlin'," Mamere says very seriously. "A girl could really fall for a boy like that."

Fall. I feel like I could fall. Just let go of all caution and good sense and just grab him and kiss him one day. But that's not the rhythm of this thing. It's like that song he was working on before, opening slowly, slowly as orange-blossom petals. "You don't go from 'What's your name?' to 'I love you' in a week," I remember Mamere chiding Mandy one time. It will take its time moving from a bud to full bloom. The anticipation is ripe and delicious, but it's still so fragile. I remember walking through the groves with Grandpere and seeing all those oranges that would never get beyond green because of a hard frost. I am taking it day by day now, feeling it come in and go out like the tides. I'm used to waiting. I'm an angler. I'm as patient as the moon.

After school the next day, I don't get quite as far toward the bus when Chase pulls up. Derek rolls down the window. "Get in," he says in a fake menacing voice. I smile and hop in without a word, sliding in next to Tru in the backseat.

"Don't you guys need a band name?" I ask when we're at Chase's house and up in his room.

"We *do* need a band name," Chase says. "Too bad 'The Beatles' is already taken."

"How about this?" I say. "Everyone contribute three names. I'll be the judge."

After about ten minutes of joking about it, I press them to submit their final three. Chase comes up with Staccato Underground, Fruit Bat Conspiracy, and A Deceit of Lapwings. "It's a real thing," he says. "You know, like a herd of cows? A bunch of lapwings is called a deceit."

"What's a lapwing?" Derek asks, looking confused.

"I don't know," says Chase. "Some kind of bird, I think. I just read it in a list of names for groups of animals."

Derek has come up with three, too: the Derek Turner Experiment, the Derek Turner Project, and the Derek Turner Experience. Tru's contributions are the Uptown Howlers, Gumbo Night, and the Thursday Night All-Stars.

"This was a tough call," I say after a reality-show-style dramatic pause. "All of these names were worthy. So I think I'm going to use part of all of them. Your new band name is Underground All-Stars Project." They applaud.

The energy level in the music room seems a little higher, and the guys practice with more focus than they did before. When we're getting ready to leave, Chase's mom comes home again. She mentions an upcoming weekend at the lake with Chase, and it's clear that Derek and Tru are going with them. "Evangeline," says Carol, "would you like to join us?"

I freeze. "Um, that would be great," I mumble. "But . . ." I trail off. This has taken me completely by surprise.

"Oh, don't worry," she says, reaching out and touching my hand. "You wouldn't be the only girl. Chase's cousin Sophie is coming with a friend. They're freshmen at the University of Georgia. I can chat with your parents if you like. I'm sure they'd feel better about it if they knew there was parental supervision."

How awkward will that conversation be? Very.

Carol calls later that night, and I can hear Mama's half of

132

the conversation. I think she is happy that rich people have asked me to their lake house. "Well, that would be just fine. Thank you for inviting her," I hear her say. What a relief.

"She seems like a nice woman," says Mama.

"She is."

"And that boy, her son, he's really just a friend?"

"He's just a friend," I say, careful not to mention anyone else who will be there.

I babysit for Aunt Cel's neighbors the next night, so I sleep over there.

"You're starting to make a life here," Mamere says while I'm brushing her hair before bed, and the words hit me like a knife to the heart. No. That's not it. I'm not making a life here. I'm going home. But I know the reason her words hurt is that there's some truth to them. She has named that feeling, the guilt I have for enjoying the last few weeks. The way it is slowly tugging me away from my resolve to be home. To rebuild the place I love.

"It's not that," I say unconvincingly. "I'm just making the best of how things are." It's that pebble-in-my-shoe feeling again. All I can think about is Danielle. If I "make a life" here, as Mamere says, it feels like I'm forgetting about her.

"That's what making a life is, *cherie,*" says Mamere. "Everything is changing all the time, and that's the way it should be. You know, when your Grandpere died—oh,

Lord. The love of my life was gone. I didn't think I could go on. But you came to live with me, and now look at us. I wouldn't miss this for the world. Doesn't mean I miss him any less."

"Do you ever think about staying in Houston?" I ask Kendra when I talk to her later.

"Hell no," she answers. "First of all, the scholarship competition is much worse here."

She's so single-minded about basketball, about college. I've always wished I could be more like her. But that's not me.

Later, when I'm reading *Evangeline,* a line jumps out at me. It's after the Acadians have been expelled from their home in Canada and they are just starting to arrive in Louisiana. Evangeline is separated from her love, Gabriel, and missing home, but from there in her boat, she's taken by the "inexpressible sweetness" of this new place. She looks around and notices everything. Above her is the Louisiana sky. Below is its reflection in the water. She is there in her boat, suspended in the middle, "hanging between two skies."

I can't help but feel like that Evangeline, hanging between two skies: the endless, inexpressibly sweet one at home and the one here, where the dark clouds are now edged by silver.

* * *

We leave for the lake house Friday after school. It's as big as their *house* house. It sleeps eighteen, Chase tells me. There's a grand piano here, too. I get my own room with this big cushy bed. Carol brought up a bunch of prepared food from some market and sets it out for us. "Chase's dad is the cook in our house. He'll be here soon," she says. I look around at the expensive stove and double oven. Mama and Mamere would die to have a kitchen like this.

We walk down to the dock with Chase. There's a little chill in the air, but it's not really cold yet. I breathe in the smell of the lake. It's not the same as salt water, but it's water. The leaves have mostly all turned or fallen off. I have to admit, it's beautiful here.

On top of the dock, there's practically another whole house, screened in, with really nice furniture and a refrigerator and sink. There's a set of stairs that leads down to the dock. Here, there's a Jet Ski, two kayaks, and a canoe. The big motorboat has been dry-docked for the winter.

"Are there fish in this lake?" Tru asks.

"Hmm. Not really sure. I think so."

Tru points over at the fall of rods and reels. "Have you ever used those?"

Chase grimaces. "I don't think *anyone* has ever used those. But you can."

Tru looks at me. "Want to go fishing tomorrow?"

My heart leaps. "Of course," I say.

135

"The boat's been—what do you call it? Winterized, though," says Chase. "I don't think you can get it down."

"We can take the canoe," says Tru.

"You know how to operate one of those?" Chase asks.

Tru looks over at me and smiles. "We both drive forty-five-foot shrimp boats. I think we can handle it."

When we come back up to the house, Chase's dad, Eric, is in the kitchen cooking, a glass of red wine on the counter. Chase's cousin Sophie and her friend Claire arrive a little while later. They're kind of the anti-Mandy, wearing mismatched clothes that look stylish together, no makeup, messy hair. We sit down at a feast of a dinner, with the fire blazing in the other room, jazz on the incredible sound system. I've never been in a scene remotely like this before. I'm terrified that someone is going to realize I'm too poor to be here. I think Tru might be feeling the same way. Derek, on the other hand, seems right at home. "I could really get used to this," he says after he polishes off a huge slab of cake.

We head down to the dock house once the dishes are done. The girls are there already, and I can smell that they've been smoking pot. They're sitting in the dark with their feet up on the tables.

"Hey!" says Sophie. "Want some?" She offers it to Tru and me.

"No, thanks," says Tru. "I'm high on life."

I shake my head.

Sophie moves on to Derek. He gives her a shocked

expression. "Are you kidding?" he says. "My lungs are like a finely tuned engine. A Ferrari. I can't damage that priceless machine with smoke."

"OK, Mr. Ferrari Lungs." Sophie laughs. "I know you'll have some, cuz."

"Yeah," says Chase. "Because you're the one who corrupted me in the first place."

Tru brought his guitar down. Everyone starts making requests and he honors them to the best of his ability. After a while, bleary-eyed Chase notices that his parents have lit a fire in the outdoor fire pit. "Oh, look," he says. "A fire. That means s'mores." He gets up and heads out with Sophie and Claire, who has been flirting with Derek. Derek follows along. But Tru lingers. I feel this joy spreading over me. He lingers because of me, I think.

"How 'bout this?" he says. "This place." He shakes his head. "I never thought I'd be in a place like this."

"Me neither," I say. And I tell him what I was thinking at the dinner table.

"I was thinking that, too!" he exclaims. "You don't think Chase is just hanging out with us for the novelty of having poor friends, do you?"

"I think Chase is just excited to *have* friends," I say. "I mean, he's great. But he's kind of an acquired taste."

He strums his guitar and starts singing a Howling Wolf song that was on one of the CDs he made me; it's about a poor boy, with no happy home to go back to.

We laugh a little and then we're silent. "That's for sure," he says.

"You mean you don't have a home to go to, or the one you do have isn't happy?"

"Things are not so great with my dad's cousins. It's their house and they're giving my dad work, but you know. He wants to be his own boss again."

"It's the same with my dad," I say. "I mean, he doesn't like to accept charity. He wants to be back out on the water again, but we have to wait for a trailer and the insurance payment for the boat. My mom just wants to stay here."

"What do you want to do?" he asks.

I was afraid he'd ask. Because if I tell him, I'm saying I want to be where he is not. "I just always thought we would go home," I say. "I mean, obviously I don't belong here."

He nods. "Yeah, I know what you mean."

My stomach is in knots. "What about you?" I manage to croak, not really wanting to know the answer.

"I don't know." I can tell he feels some of what I'm feeling. "I don't really have a choice in the matter. We're here now. And there are some good things about it." He gives me a look as if he is about to say more, but the screen door swings open and Chase walks in.

"Come on," he says, sounding loopy with a mouth full of marshmallows. "You're missing the s'mores."

We sit around the fire, under the blankets that Carol and Eric brought out. Claire and Sophie have gotten over their case of the giggles and are looking a little glassy eyed. There's jazz coming from the speakers mounted on the trees, and the sky is so clear. You can see tons of stars. It's like a dream. But in my heart, in my head, there's a voice. Not even a little one. A strong and sure one, that says, *You don't belong here.* And I know it's right. This place is amazing. But it's not *my* place. It's not my home.

It's still dark out the next morning when there is a knock on my door. I'm not sure where I am at first, but I fumble around, find the handle. Tru is outside, and for a split second, I think he wants to come into my bedroom, and I have a moment of panic. But he puts his fingers to his lips to say *shhh* and mimics casting a line, and I realize he has woken me up to go fishing. I nod, give him the "just a second" sign and go get dressed. When I come out, he has assembled some sandwiches for lunch. He holds up some chicken. "This is all we've got for bait."

I scrawl a note and leave it on the counter: *Gone fishin'.*

It's cold and black out when we head to the dock and collect the rods and reels. There's a thick mist coming off the water. "Do you know where we're going?" I ask as we start to paddle out.

"No idea," he says.

"I'm starting to see a pattern here. Out on the water with no sense of direction and no navigational equipment," I say.

"Ouch," he says. "Well played."

"Just kidding. How big can this lake be?"

We paddle out as the dark begins to soften. That peace comes over me. A flock of geese fly in formation above us, their barely audible honks echoing across the lake. They'll be arriving in Louisiana soon, I think, remembering this time of year at home. It would just about be orange-harvest season, too, just a few weeks before the festival. But almost all the oranges are dead this year.

"You're quiet back there," says Tru from the front of the canoe. "What are you thinking about?"

I tell him. "I was thinking about home, too," he says. He tells me that he used to come to the Orange Festival every year. His little sister wanted to be on the court one day.

"I think my sister is more upset about not being on Orange Court than she is about losing our house," I say. "My mom was on the court when she was in high school."

"So not only are you Fleet Queen, but you're orange royalty, too? Man, who cares if Chase is rich? You're royal."

"Yep. My blood runs orange."

"You know, I asked my cousin Hip about you," he says. "After we met that day."

"You did?" I'm terrified at what Hip might have said. Probably "Who?" and then "Oh, Mandy Riley's little sister?"

"He said you were cool," he says.

"He did not say that."

"Well, he said that he knew you were the one who always won the fishing rodeos. So I'm a little intimidated going fishing with you."

"Yeah, you should be. Totally."

We decide to try the banks, since we know nothing about this lake. But everything seems to be private property. We finally find this little island and haul out just as my arms are starting to get tired of paddling.

At first, there's this nervous energy. I feel like I have to show off and catch something right away.

"Ah, I see you have a slight flick," he says. "Is it trademarked?"

"Don't even attempt it. You may injure yourself."

We fish. The conversation ebbs and flows like tides. It starts to develop a rhythm, like a waltz, sometimes quick and witty, sometimes slower, deeper, more reflective.

"When you're fishing like this," he says, "do you ever imagine that you're on a fishing show, like *Bassmasters*? And narrate what you're doing?"

"You do that, too?"

"Yeah, you can be a guest star on my show today." He puts on a redneck announcer voice. "Today, we're here with Evangeline Riley, five-time Bayou Perdu Fishing Rodeo champion, who's going to show us how to bank fish in North Georgia —"

"Hey, what's your show called? *Tru Bayou?*"

"Good one." He puts his announcer voice back on. "We'd like to welcome Evangeline Riley to *Tru Bayou* today. Evangeline, tell me how you do it."

"Well, Tru, you have to think like a fish. . . ."

The day is warming up. There are other boats out fishing. We move to different spots around the island. Not surprisingly, we catch nothing with chicken. We decide to have lunch. Light is coming through the trees on the little island, soft and warm. He says his brothers are studying business at LSU and the idea was that when they graduate, they were going to start Nguyen Brothers Seafood Enterprises. Not just fishing, but distribution. He was going to join them after school and pursue his music on the side. But now . . . Who knows how long it will take to save for a new boat?

It gets too warm to fish, so we head back. He's in front of me in the boat, looking out over the water with his hair blowing in the wind, the billowy clouds in front of him. I feel this image of him imprinting on my memory, as if years from now, I'll always remember him exactly this way.

He helps me out of the boat onto the dock. A strand of my hair falls, and he reaches over and pushes it back, his hand warm, strong, but soft. A shiver runs through me, the way an egret's feathers ripple slightly in the wind as it's about to take flight.

When we get back up to the back deck, Chase is still in his robe, hanging out with Sophie. "Oh, God," he deadpans. "We thought you had capsized."

"We didn't really think that," Sophie says. "We just woke up."

"Where are all the fish you caught us for lunch?" Chase asks.

"Well, we didn't have any actual bait," says Tru.

"We can get some," says Chase. "We need to go to the general store anyway. A terrible thing has happened. We're out of coffee."

We take the little country road to the store and pick up some bait, the coffee, and a few other things, and I'm standing at the cashier with Chase when I turn around and there's Tate. His jaw drops. Mine probably does, too.

"Evangeline! What are you doing here?"

"Just up here for the weekend." Why do I feel guilty? I turn to Chase. "With friends."

Tate looks at Chase. "Hey," he says. Even though Tate would probably never show disdain to anyone, I can tell that he knows Chase and doesn't like him.

"Well, see you at school," I say as we head out to the car. For some reason, I feel like I've been caught doing something I'm not supposed to do.

"You know Tate?" I ask Chase when we're back in the car.

"Not really. We went to preschool together. I think we went to each other's birthday parties until we were, like, five. How do you know him?"

"Political Science."

143

"He's harmless," says Chase. "Just a little uptight."

The afternoon is dreamy. We eat lunch out on the deck. It's warm and sunny. There is a football game on in the living room that Derek, Claire, Sophie, and Eric are watching. Carol is reading a book. I get in the hammock near the lake and stare out at the water. After about ten minutes, Tru comes down. "Mind if I join you?" he asks.

For a second, I think he's going to get in right next to me, but he goes to the other end and we swing there, the way Kendra and I used to do. I tell him about her. He tells me his older brother, Than, is his best friend and adds, "It would be cool if you could meet him sometime." It's the first hint that he is starting to see me in his future. That tiny little voice in the back of my head chimes in: *But you don't belong here.* I brush it aside.

I tell him about Danielle. That we're best friends, that we've been each other's anchor for years. And then in one day, she was just swept away.

"I feel like this limbo we're all in is just temporary," he says. "It might take some time, but I know you two will find each other. This being apart doesn't erase all the years you spent together."

"Her life in Bayou Perdu was never great, though. Maybe they just moved on. Maybe she doesn't want to remember."

"I don't believe that's it. The friendship you just described seems stronger than that."

In this time that we are here together, sandwiched between two trees, our bodies thrown together, I study the details of him: his hands, the line of his cheekbones, the exact color of his eyes. What would it be called? Chestnut? It's a warm brown, not ordinary. It's a brown that's just his, almost a honey, golden brown. I have started zeroing in on his lips. I have to stop because the line between looking at them and wanting to lunge at him and kiss them has grown dangerously thin. All those clichés about love: it turns out they're true.

Later, there is another incredible dinner, and afterward everyone gathers in the living room this time. Eric lights a fire and everyone gets under blankets and unzipped sleeping bags.

"I would love to hear some New Orleans music," says Carol. "Since we've got two New Orleans musicians here with us."

Derek offers to play "Basin Street Blues." Tru begs off, so he does it with Chase. When they're done, Carol says, "Derek! Amazing. I had no idea you were such an accomplished musician!" He shrugs a little. But not too much.

Carol is quizzing him on his musical background. "Have you ever thought of applying to a conservatory?" she asks.

"I was supposed to go to this academy in New Orleans," he says. "Before Katrina."

"He should audition at Manhattan, don't you think, Chase? We know some people in admissions."

"He can have my old spot," says Chase, sounding a little bitter.

Tru picks up his guitar and sits on the edge of the fireplace. There's something in his voice when he begins. It takes me a second to recognize that he's singing Louis Armstrong's "A Kiss to Build a Dream On."

He is looking straight out over the room for almost the whole song, but he catches my eye for a second and smiles. I feel myself blushing.

"Absolutely stunning," says Carol when he's finished. "Chase, your friends here are as talented as your friends at Manhattan were."

"What can I say? I attract talent," he says.

Tru comes and sits next to me.

"Wow," I squeak out. "That was amazing."

He shrugs. "It seemed like the right time for that song."

The song was a tough act to follow, so no one does. Sophie, Claire, and Derek start playing Trivial Pursuit. Chase wanders off to his room. I help Chase's mom with the cleaning up. When I finish, Tru, who has been in the living room messing around on the guitar, comes in to join us.

"Do you want to go outside?" he asks. I can barely breathe. This is the tug on my line. This is it.

We walk out beyond the squares of light spilling from the house. When we pass into the darkness, Tru grabs my hand. We walk down to the dock together that way. My thinking breaks down. Stars, the chill in the air, that smell of lake water, his hand in mine. My mind has slowed to a crawl and it's only my senses. His hand in mine. I think words are coming from my mouth, but I couldn't tell you what I'm saying. Now we're face-to-face. Eye to eye. I could lift off the ground, I'm so light.

And then he is kissing me and I'm kissing back.

He breathes out and pulls me close to him. "I kissed the Fleet Queen!" he says, his face beaming. "I've wanted to do that since the day we met."

"Why didn't you?" I ask.

"I was scared, of course," he says. "I thought you would laugh. Or leave me out there."

"I was covered in water and smelling like fish. Why would you want to kiss me?"

"The shrimp crown really caught my eye, you know, earlier in the day." He tilts his head back and laughs. "Seriously, though, I noticed your looks first. But then it was your superpowers. You just jumped right into alligator-infested waters and set me free and that was it. Boom. Lightning bolts." Kiss. "Then there's your sense of humor." Kiss. "Confidence. The way you sing in French. Everything, basically." Kiss. "What about you? When was the first time you knew you wanted to kiss me?"

"It was pretty much the same time." We're kissing again. We go into the dock house to be alone, settle down under the unzipped sleeping bag that someone left out there last night. I can't really say what happened next. Talking, kissing, a soft blur like that song that took me so far away to someplace I've never been. A place I want to visit again and again. It's like the wings of this big white bird spread out and then settle over me. I'm so close to this beautiful, fragile thing—this feeling. I've been close to it before, but didn't want to get nearer. Like I was afraid any movement would scare it away. But now I feel like I belong. Here. With him. We go back in when we see the lights start to go out inside the house. He drops me off at my door like a gentleman and says good night. I can't sleep. I feel like I just woke up. For the first time ever.

During breakfast, Chase senses what's going on. And since Derek and Claire have disappeared, I think he's feeling like a third wheel. "You know, when I invited you guys up here, I had no idea this was going to turn into the love hotel." He puts his coffee cup down on the table just a little too hard.

In the afternoon, everything is sort of fuzzy. We all play card games with Chase and Sophie for a while. Tru brushes up against me a few times and I feel electrified. I can't seem to focus on anything but him. Later, we break up into smaller groups. We both spend time with Chase alone, out of guilt for me, at least. Then Tru and I have a few minutes alone on the back deck. I am dying to kiss him and wondering if he is thinking the same thing. But there are people just on the other side of the glass. Then it's time to head back.

When Chase drops me off at Aunt Cel's at the end of the day, I say good-bye to Tru in the backseat, but then he gets out and comes around the back of the car. "Wait, we need to have a real good-bye." He touches my shoulder, then puts his hand on my hip, pulling me closer to kiss him, a kiss that goes right through me. I'm like a leaf that fell into the water, picked up into his flow, gliding along with it. I forget who and where I am and I'm liquid. I could float away, evaporate.

"Oh, God, you two, get a room," Chase moans out the car window.

I have to pull myself back to stay in my own skin, but the feeling echoes as the car pulls away.

As I'm going to bed that night, I think about Mandy's stupid advice about dating. For me so far, falling in love has been nothing like fishing. It is more like making music. Trying to find a melody and matching the words, and then when they're together, getting lost in it. Carried away. You carry it in your body so that sometimes it bursts out of you and other times it's quiet and so unconscious that you're humming and you don't even notice it. It's that slow unfurling of the orange bud. And now I am that tiny orange bud bursting into blossom.

The Long Pause

THE WEEK AFTER THE LAKE WEEKEND, the rehearsals at Chase's are a little unfocused. They break up early. Chase skulks into his room, Derek goes downstairs to fix himself a snack and sit in front of the TV. Tru and I stay in Chase's music room, with the big stack of his dad's records from the '70s and '80s and the turntable, examining the pictures and delicately dropping the needle on the tracks we want to listen to. Lou Reed, the Velvet Underground, Gram Parsons, other musicians that people have forgotten about singing songs of love.

We are sitting on the floor, heads close together. My brain shuts off. I'm just feeling. All I am aware of is him, sparks coming from the closeness of us together, and then we are kissing again.

I never expected to feel this away about kissing. How it becomes a hunger in you, a craving. It's not all I think about, but on the days when we see each other but don't have any time alone together, I have a kind of dull ache and burning impatience to be alone with him again. He is the first thing I think of when I wake up in the morning and the last thing I think of before I go to sleep at night.

Mandy has figured out that something is going on with me. I catch her eyeing me suspiciously when we're doing homework in our room one night. "There's something different about you," she says.

"Like what?"

"I can't put my finger on it." Then she has a revelation. "You're happy. That's it."

"Happy? That's different?"

"Uh, yeah. You've met someone, haven't you?"

I hesitate, but I can't help telling her. "Yes."

She smiles. Come to think of it, I haven't seen her smile in a long time, either. "Details, please," she says.

"Well, he's from St. Bernard. I actually met him before. At the Blessing. He's Hip Tran's cousin."

"Oh." She looks slightly confused. "But I mean, what does he *look* like? What is he into?"

"He looks . . ." I don't know how to describe it. "Cool. He's into music. He plays guitar."

Her eyes go wide. She nods. "Not bad. And he's nice to you?"

"Very."

"Have you kissed him yet? Oh, God, you have—I can tell. Why didn't you tell me?" She is excited. This whole time, I thought she would be the last person I'd tell about Tru. But it feels good to tell her. I feel closer to her than I have in a long time. I don't have Danielle. I don't have Kendra. I don't have a best friend anymore. But I do have a sister.

One afternoon, Derek's home sick, and when we get to Chase's house, he says he's really tired and may be getting sick, too. "I'm just going to lie down for a while," he says, heading up the stairs. "You can hang out or take the car if you want. Just be back by around seven so my mom doesn't freak out." He tosses Tru the keys.

In Chase's car, we look at each other and laugh.

"Should we just take it and drive back to New Orleans?" He gives me a conspiratorial look. "We could live in this thing. It's actually nicer than where I'm living now."

The idea of us running away together hangs in the air for a moment. "I'm up for it," I say.

We have three hours and a car. What will we do?

Neither of us really knows where we're going. We just get out on that big ugly road near our school, punching at the car radio, looking for something to listen to. A girl and boy in secondhand clothes, in a borrowed car, riding down an ugly strip. But I feel like I'm bouncing off the clouds. I put my hand on the window and feel the cold from the glass seep into me, the gloom of early December on the other side of it kept at bay by the warmth, the closeness, inside Chase's fancy car, the two of us together.

Tru settles on some Mexican station playing cheesy love songs in Spanish, which neither of us can understand. The announcers are reading out phone numbers in booming, over-the-top voices: *ceh-ro, ceh-ro, cin-co.* A rhythmic, accordion-heavy song comes on, not too different from zydeco, really. It has a catchy chorus; we both pick it up pretty quickly, singing with mock earnestness.

"Maybe this can be our song," he says. "You know how couples are supposed to have a song that's their song? We don't have a song."

This surge of happiness wells up in me. We're a *we.*

"Tell you what," he says. "I'm going to write a song for us. A song for you, actually. I'll play it onstage tomorrow."

I hide my face in my hands. "Oh, God. OK."

"What? Are you nervous?"

"Shy."

"Superhero Gumbo Girl? No way."

"I don't like attention."

"I wouldn't ever do anything to embarrass you. You know that, right?"

I nod.

"Music is just my way to express things I can't say any other way," he explains. His eyes are intent on the road. "Do you have any money?" he asks suddenly.

I scrounge in my pants pocket. "About thirteen bucks." There are a few more cents in my backpack.

"Should we get something to eat?"

"Sure." We're on that ugly strip of road with a zillion Asian restaurants and businesses. He pulls into Chinatown Mall.

"There's a place here where we could probably swing it."

It's just an ordinary restaurant with plastic-covered seats and tile floors, a few fake plants, and pictures of scenic places in Vietnam on the wall. We order a bowl of pho—which Tru says is great and enough for two—and some spring rolls. The waiter doesn't seem very pleased about our meager order. Tru tells me about his mom's pho, which he says is the best, and I tell him about the diner. "That's your mom's restaurant? I've been there!" he exclaims. He describes his waitress, and we realize that it was probably Mandy. What if I had been there, in the kitchen, and we hadn't even known it? What if there were lots of times when we'd been so close to meeting?

The pho is comforting. It's different from my family's home cooking, but it makes me feel the same way: full and cared for.

We walk around the stores in the strip mall. There's a grocery store with all kinds of imported goods. Spiky fruits and pungent herbs. We pick up some fabric dye and a four-pack of men's white T-shirts that I promise to make into really cool shirts for the band to wear at the concert. "Since I'm the groupie," I say.

There's a gift store with little Japanese erasers shaped like desserts and animals. They have a photo booth that prints your faces on sticky film with designs on it, and we have just enough cash to get our picture taken. I sit on Tru's lap. We adjust ourselves, facing the blinking red eye of the camera before the flash goes off. Awkward exchanges. "I think my eyes were closed." "I look like I'm possessed." The flash goes off again. Right before the last one, I lean into him and he puts his cheek on mine and the camera catches both of us with looks on our faces that say, "I am so lucky to be with this person." The machine spits out the tiny, almost impossible-to-see images of us on the sticker-print bodies of animals: we're giraffes and ecstatic, in-love elephants. He rips the strip of pictures in half so we each get some.

"I wish I could take you somewhere on a real date," he says when we've finished our sweep of the mall and are back in Chase's car. "Someplace nice."

"This *was* nice," I say. "This was perfect."

He drops me off at Aunt Cel's house so I can go to my babysitting gig. We have one more kiss, intense, no looking away. We don't even say good-bye. When I get home from babysitting, I stay up late working on the band T-shirts, gray dye in the sink, potato-print letters and stars. I'm dazed with happiness.

It's a little awkward the next day at school. Things are hurried. I give him the T-shirt. He grins and holds it up in front of him. "Excellent," he says. "Another hidden talent I didn't know you had: T-shirt designer."

The concert is tonight and the guys are busy with last-minute rehearsals, so we don't really have any time together. But I got Mandy to agree to drive me. "I guess I'll stay so I don't have to drive you back and forth," she says with a sigh.

"Chase can drive me home." I don't want her there. I'm practically out of my body with excitement about this night. My night. My song.

She scowls at me. "Fine. I don't want to be seen at that place anyway."

After dinner, I've got my Underground All-Stars Project shirt on and I am just about to walk out the door when the phone rings. It's Aunt Cel. There's something strange and serious in her voice. "Turn on the TV right now," she urges. "On the public TV station. It's Danielle."

It's a documentary called *Deep Water,* about the lives of a group of Katrina refugees who settled in Utah. When I turn it on, they are showing that awful footage of Katrina that everyone shows — the trees bent over in the relentless wind, people waving white flags from the top of their roofs, desperate to be rescued. The scene turns to a shelter in a school gym in Baton Rouge. The camera pans around the hot, tired, desperate-looking people. "This is where we met sixteen-year-old Danielle," the announcer says. Then they cut to Danielle.

She looks so different. Her hair is perfectly cut with a headband in it. She's wearing makeup, which I've never seen her do before. She's in a dark room, talking about what happened.

"The Sunday morning before Katrina, there was almost no one left in Bayou Perdu," she says. "I started to get scared." She explains how some guy her mom worked with at the Home Depot called and asked if they wanted a ride. He wasn't sure where he was going, but he had room in his car. Desiree decided they should take him up on it. "We brought one change of clothes. That's it." The coworker drove down from Bellvoir to get them, but by the time they got to New Orleans, the roads were closing. They had to go to the shelter at the convention center. It was all right for the first night, but by the second night it was bad, and by the third it was chaos. She was one of those people waiting on the bridge to be picked up and taken to a shelter, the ones on TV. "I saw things. Things I don't want to remember." She stops for a moment. "I don't want to talk about it."

She had needed my help and I wasn't there for her.

When the bus finally did come and took them to Baton Rouge to live in a school gym, things were better there, but still. She stops again. "It was hard." I know Danielle. I can read between the lines. Desiree must have been losing it. "At first, after the storm, I couldn't feel anything. I was just in survival mode, you know? It was just getting through every hour and every minute."

The Red Cross started assigning people to long-term housing, says Danielle. They told them they'd have a new home, but they weren't sure where yet. And that's when she found out she was going to be living in Utah. Both she and Desiree were against it. They didn't even know where Utah *was.* But the Red Cross gave them plane tickets and told them they'd have their own home there. They didn't have anything to lose. So they went.

Danielle had never been on a plane before. They flew over the desert, she says. And when they landed, "it was like landing over the rainbow." The scene switches to an airport tarmac, snowy mountains in the distance. Katrina refugees are starting to disembark from a plane. There are people on the tarmac doing a second line parade to welcome them. Several of the families, says the announcer, are "adopted" by church congregations who help them start over. We see Danielle and Desiree meeting the church family who adopted them: a man called Alan, whose wife died a few years ago, and his three daughters, who seem to be in their twenties. They all walk into a new apartment that the church is paying for, Danielle looking shell-shocked and Desiree in tears. It's fully furnished; there's even a computer for Danielle. We see Danielle walking the halls of her new school, everyone being really nice to her. She starts to smile and laugh. Desiree is at her job at a warehouse, packing boxes.

It seems like they're trying to show that something is starting to happen between Alan and Desiree. Alan talks about how he hasn't had a purpose since his wife died. Helping Desiree and Danielle has made him feel needed again. Then they cut to Desiree, on the couch with a tissue in her hand. "The thing is," she says, "I wasn't a very good mother to Danielle. I've made a lot of mistakes. I've hurt a lot of people I cared about. And I could never get out of that cycle. My past was always *right there*. But here"—she chokes up—"no one judges me. I get to start over." It's a side to Desiree I've never seen before, and I feel guilty again for all the times I've been one of those people judging her.

"For some," the narrator intones, "Katrina was a blessing wrapped in a curse." They show Alan putting his arm around Desiree's shoulders.

They cut to Danielle. "When we got to Utah," she says, "I was expecting to feel terrible and alone. But it was like this big desert was between me and my old life, all the bad stuff. What was in front of me was all new, with no black marks on it yet, you know? With my mom . . ." She hesitates, but I know what she's thinking. *With my mom acting like a mom now.* "I get to be the kid now."

They cut again to church. People are singing hymns, then gathering in the fellowship hall afterward. Desiree and Danielle seem to be doing better than a lot of the other refugees. Some of them are thinking about going back to Louisiana or to Houston. Many of them lost members of their families, old people especially. "A new life means painful good-byes," the narrator says.

They cut to Danielle again. "The person I miss the most is my best friend, Evangeline," she says. "She's always been like a sister to me." She gets a little teary. "I don't know where she is now. I don't know how we'll ever see each other again." They play the instrumental part of "Do You Know What It Means to Miss New Orleans?" as they roll the credits.

My throat starts to close.

I look up to see tears running down Mama's face. She leaves the room and Daddy goes after her. Mandy reaches over and grabs my hand and squeezes it for a moment. "Are you OK?" she asks in almost a whisper. I can only shake my head.

The feelings swirling around in me range from relief (she's alive, she has a great new life, she has what she's always wanted, to just be a kid) to betrayal (how can she not want to go back home?).

The TV announcer tells people that if they want to help the refugees they've just seen or any others, there's a number they should call. I grab a pen and write it on my arm.

"Do you still want me to take you to that thing?" Mandy asks.

The concert. It went completely out of my mind. I need to see Tru. Mandy gets the car keys.

On the way, I check my phone and see that I missed four calls from Chase while I was watching the documentary. There are three voice mails.

The first is this: "Hey, where are you? We're starting in about ten minutes. Are you coming? OK, bye."

The second is: "OK, you're late. We're going on next. Where are you?"

The third is Tru on Chase's phone. "Hey, are you on your way? Pick up. Pick up. Pick up."

When I get to the event space, I can see that the concert is already over, although people are still milling about. I can't see Tru anywhere, but of course Chase's hair stands out.

"What happened to you?" he says, annoyed. "I tried to call you, like, a million times. You missed it."

I explain.

"Wow," he says.

"Where's Tru?

"Gone," he says. "You just missed him, but that's probably a good thing. After we played, I saw him in the back of the room with this guy who I guess was his dad. They were arguing. Kind of loudly. In Vietnamese. He came back to where me and Derek were and grabbed his guitar, and he asked if I'd seen you yet. And I said no. He said he had to go, but to tell you he was sorry. And then he said, 'I'm not sure what's going to happen. But tell Evangeline I'll be in touch as soon as I can.' And then he left."

"Did he seem OK?"

"He seemed upset. I don't know."

"Should we go over there?" I don't know where he lives, but Chase does.

"It kind of felt like a family thing. Maybe we should let it blow over."

Part of me thinks, *What if he needs me?* But I don't say anything. "I guess we'll find out Monday."

I barely sleep that night. The next morning I call the phone number I wrote on my arm. I don't understand what the person says when she answers, but she ends with "How can I help you?"

"I saw the documentary last night. *Deep Water.* My friend was in it. I'm trying to get in touch with her."

I'm met with silence. "Did you want to donate?" the woman asks.

"No, I want to get in touch with my friend who was in the documentary."

Silence again. "I don't have that information," the woman says.

"Can you put me in touch with the people who made the film? My friend said she was looking for me. I'm looking for her." I feel increasingly irritated.

"Hold, please," the woman says.

I hold, thinking about hanging up. It seems like forever before another person comes on the line. "This is Jane Hall. Can I help you?" she asks.

"I'm Evangeline Riley. My friend Danielle was the girl in the documentary. She said she's been looking for me. And I've been looking for her."

"Hmmm," says Jane. "Can I get your number, Evangeline? I can get the producer to give you a call."

I give her the number.

"I'll have Laura get in touch with you as soon as she can and maybe she can help you find your friend," she says.

All weekend long, a cloud is hanging over me. A swirling cloud, gathering its strength.

On Monday, I go straight to Tru's homeroom. But he's not there. At lunch, he's not in music. Derek hasn't seen or heard from him, either.

"I can drive you to his house after school," Chase says.

He drops off Derek, then heads down the big commercial road to where there are some run-down apartments. He pulls into one right next to the highway.

Bayou Perdu is poor, but this is a different kind of poor. An urban kind of poor that has a different edge to it.

"This is where I always drop him off," Chase says. "He's never invited me up. But it's the last one on the end upstairs."

"Do you want to come with me?" I ask.

"I can, but it's OK if you want to talk to him alone," he says. "I get it. Third wheel here."

I walk up the concrete steps to the second floor alone, feeling shaky. I take a deep breath before I knock on the door. There's no response. I try again, a little louder. The curtain of the window near the door moves aside and a woman looks out at me suspiciously, then closes the curtain again. In a moment, I can hear the door unlock, and she opens it just a crack.

"Hi," I say. "I'm looking for Tru. I'm a friend from school."

She scowls at me and shakes her head and says something in Vietnamese. I feel my face flush.

She shouts at someone in the apartment and a girl, probably around twelve years old, appears. She also looks at me a little warily.

"Hi," I say. "I'm Evangeline. I'm a friend of Tru's. Is he here?"

She shakes her head.

"Oh. OK. Well, when he comes back, can you tell him that I stopped by?"

"He doesn't live here anymore," she says quietly.

"Oh. Do you know where they moved to?"

The girl shakes her head. She looks fearful.

"I don't know," she says. "I think they went back to Louisiana. That's what Uncle said."

Her words hit me like a punch in the stomach.

"Louisiana?"

She nods.

"Where in Louisiana?"

She shakes her head. "I heard them say Baton Rouge. But I don't know." The girl looks like she's going to cry. "There was an argument," she says. "They took all their things and left."

I can't breathe. I start down the stairs as fast as I can, trying to catch my breath.

When I get to the car, I slam the door.

"Are you OK?" Chase asks.

I shake my head.

"Just take a deep breath," he says. "Tell me what happened."

I try and nothing comes out. I can't breathe.

He rolls down the car window to give me some air. I feel it on my face, but I still can't speak. He starts the car. "OK," he says. "Let's get outta here."

The car starts to move and somehow it loosens my

words. "He's gone," I say. "This kid—his cousin, I guess—said he went back to Louisiana."

"Are you serious?" asks Chase.

I can only nod.

"Wow," he says. Then the car falls into an awful silence. "Maybe that's what the argument was about Friday. Do you want me to take you home?" he asks.

I shake my head.

"OK," he says.

As we drive, I keep going over it again and again in my mind. There must be a mistake.

We get to a taco place and sit down. Chase goes to get food, then puts a basket of chips in front of me.

"You're going to have to speak again sometime," he says.

I say nothing.

"Have a chip," he says.

I take one and start eating mechanically.

"I should have been there Friday night," I say. "If I had been there . . ."

"It wouldn't have changed anything," he says. "His dad was really upset. There's nothing you could have done."

"There was a song he was going to play," I say. "It was important. He wrote it for me."

"He didn't play it," says Chase.

"Because I wasn't there."

"Well, you needed to find out about your best friend. Tru would understand that."

"I didn't get to say good-bye."

"He'll be in touch."

"How? He doesn't have a phone."

"It's not like we live in the Dark Ages. He can find a way."

Think. I just have to think. I need to figure out a way to reach him.

"Look," says Chase. "He didn't break up with you. He just left, and not of his own accord. Just remember that."

I nod. Who would have thought Chase would be so good at calming someone down?

When he drops me off, Chase says, "Sorry, kid. You know what Shakespeare said. The course of true love never did run smooth. Ha. 'Tru' love. Get it?"

I get out of the car. There is still a possibility, I tell myself, that that girl was wrong. Maybe they've just moved to a new apartment in Atlanta. I'll hear from him.

But days go by. Days. And he doesn't turn up. It is slowly sinking in. He's gone.

I stop going to the music room at lunch to see if he's there. The next day Chase shows up at my lunch. "What am I, chopped liver?" he asks.

I pull out my earbuds.

"You're not going to come to music anymore because Tru is gone? It was all about him?"

"That's not it," I say. "I just don't want to be reminded that he's not there."

"Well, come on, then," he says. "I need someone to counterbalance Derek's ego."

Being with them helps a little. Even though we don't talk about him, they are the thread that connects me to Tru.

"You have to quit moping," says Chase one afternoon while he's driving me home. "Look, when I got kicked out of the best music school in the country, I felt like a huge disappointment to everyone in my life. But it's temporary. Something else is coming for you. Right now, you're in what we call a *fermata* in music. A long pause. You have to hold that note for a while longer. But then you go on to the rest of the composition. Just wait it out."

At home a new tension hangs over the house, a gathering of vapors, swirling itself into a storm. It's the week of the Orange Festival back home. For a while, it seemed like they weren't going to have it this year. But in a show of Plaquemines strength and resilience, they decided to do it anyway. The court is always chosen in September, but this year they had to wait for people to come back. It's mostly girls from Bellvoir who had been allowed to move back into their houses. But there were two girls from Bayou Perdu High School, both cheerleading friends of Mandy's. After one of them called to let her know that she made it, you could tell it was eating Mandy up. Then on Monday they announced the queen. It's a girl from Bellvoir. We see her picture in the *Times-Picayune* online, holding her orange scepter in her white-gloved hands, these beaded things that look like wings coming out of the top of her dress. "Her?" Mandy spits. "Seriously? Obviously there wasn't much competition."

"You would have picked a much better dress." I meant it to be supportive, but she gives me a poisonous look.

But a few days later, she gets an early Christmas present. Byron calls. He's broken up with that girl, Elena. He misses Mandy. He wants to get back together. He wants to come down to Atlanta during winter break. She acts put out at first, but I know this is the best news she's had in a long time. Someone wants her. They're on the phone all the time, every night, keeping me awake. It's annoying until I realize that Byron is friends with Hip, and Hip might know where Tru is.

"Ask him for Hip's number," I demand before she gets on the phone one night.

"Right, Evangeline. We *just* got back together and I'm going to ask him for his friend's number. Are you joking?"

Joking? No. I'm desperate. So one night when she's on the phone with Byron, I make my move. I grab the phone right out of her hand. As I'm fending her off with one arm, I start talking.

"Byron? Hey, this is Evangeline."

"Oh, hey, little sister" comes Byron's smooth, cocky voice over the line. "What's up?"

"Listen, I know you were friends with Hip Tran, and I was wondering if you know where he is now."

"Hipppp Traaaan," Byron says in that way that makes everyone's name sound like some sort of a statement. "The Hipster. Hippie. You know, we haven't been in touch, but I think I heard he's in Houston now. Most people are. I'm not sure."

"You don't happen to have his phone number, do you?"

"Hang on," he says. Mandy is swatting at me, trying to get the phone back. Byron is pushing random buttons. "Whoops, hang on. How do you check numbers while you're on the phone?" He presses a few more. "The Hipster. Yeah, I got his digits. You ready?"

My heart may beat out of my chest. I lunge at the desk, papers flying everywhere as I fumble for a pen. "OK, go ahead."

He reads out a 504 number.

"Fantastic. Thank you so much, Byron. I guess I'll see you in a few weeks."

Mandy punches me in the arm as I give her the phone back.

I sit on the concrete step out front to call Hip. Breathe deep. I dial the number. It rings three, four times. I figure it's going to go to voice mail when he picks up on the fifth ring. I'm petrified.

"Hello?"

"Hi. Um, Hip?"

"Yeah?"

"This is Evangeline Riley. From Bayou Perdu High? Mandy Riley's little sister."

"Oh. Right. Yeah. Hi." He sounds confused but blasé about hearing from me, as if random girls call him out of the blue all the time.

"I'm sorry to bother you. Byron Delacroix gave me your number." I'm sure he's confused. "I was wondering if you knew how to get in touch with your cousin Tru. We know each other from Atlanta. But he left, and I just need to get in touch with him." This is awkward beyond all description.

"Oh, yeah, Tru. I heard they were in Atlanta."

"But not anymore," I say. "They left and your other cousins—I mean, I don't know if they are cousins on your side—the people they were living with said they went back to Louisiana. I was just wondering if you knew where. And how to get in touch. It's just—no one else I know knows them."

"I didn't know they weren't in Atlanta anymore. That's the last I heard. Hmm. That's weird. I can ask my dad."

"Oh, great. Thanks."

"Well, he's at work now. Do me a favor. Can you call me back? I'm terrible at remembering things."

"Sure. Of course. When would be good?"

"Maybe on the weekend?"

"Sure. Sorry." This is painful.

"OK, then," he says. "That's funny, you know. He asked me about you at the Blessing of the Fleet."

"Yeah," I say. "We met there. Then we ran into each other again here in Atlanta." *And fell in love,* I want to say. "So thanks for asking your dad. I'll check back with you on the weekend."

"OK," he says before hanging up.

That was excruciating, but I finally feel like I'm getting somewhere.

I call again on the weekend and, amazingly, he picks up.

"Hi, Hip," I say, desperate to get this awkward conversation over with. "It's Evangeline Riley. I wondered if you'd had a chance to talk to your dad about the Nguyens yet?"

"Oh, hey," he says. "Yeah, I asked my mom. She was surprised. She said she didn't know where they were, and then she started crying. She's upset about the family all getting moved around and all, you know? But we're going to see Tru's dad's other cousin at Christmas, so they should know. Do you want to just call me again after Christmas? Like I said, I'm terrible at remembering things."

"Sure. Thanks for your help. And can I just give you my number in case you hear from him?"

He says that he'll save my number, but I have my doubts.

* * *

At Christmas, Mama picks up one of those small fake trees that's already decorated and plugs it in on a table in the living room. We have Christmas Day at Aunt Cel's house. She buys us tons of stuff. I think it only makes Mama feel worse because her presents aren't as impressive. She pitches a defense for each of the presents as the recipient opens it. "I thought you could use it for your new apartment, Ami," or "Oh, it was on sale. I thought it was cute." My cousin Ami overdoes it, too, with her *oohs* and *ahs*. "I love it!" she squeals over the most inconsequential things. The whole day is uncomfortable. Daddy looks blank, the way he usually does now. I sit next to him and put my head on his shoulder. He strokes my hair. "Merry Christmas, baby," he says with a weak smile.

I sneak off to Ami's bedroom because I just don't feel like being with other people. I'm staring into space when Mandy finds me.

"What are you doing in here?"

"Nothing. Just thinking."

"About what?"

"Last Christmas. Danielle."

"And Tru?"

"Yeah."

"Look," she says. "Things can turn around. Look at me. I thought I'd never hear from Byron again, and now things are better than ever. Just come on down, there's a present we haven't opened yet that will make you happy."

I reluctantly follow her downstairs. It's the annual box of pralines we got from Delbert, Mrs. Menil's son, who took the trouble to find out where we are. His mother is living with him Uptown in New Orleans now since only the steps remained on her house. *Fifty years of our family history was completely destroyed,* he wrote in his note. *But we'll never forget what good neighbors you always were, and even though we're far apart, I hope I can find some way to return all the favors you did for Mama and me through the years.*

Byron comes down from Nashville the day after Christmas and stays over at Aunt Cel's house so she can "keep an eye on him." It's strangely good to see him. Like a little piece of wreckage that's left from Bayou Perdu. We talk about people we know, even if we don't know them well. He and Mandy are all lovey-dovey. For the first day. They're talking about LSU next year, when they can be together again. Mandy's got her application in, she says, and is feeling confident. She's even signed up to try out for softball in the spring at Brookdale in case that improves her chances. But by the second afternoon, Mandy seems to be stomping around. Daddy and Byron are watching the game in the living room by themselves. Later, I see Mandy and Byron standing at the end of the driveway, obviously fighting.

By the third morning, he's gone. Mandy won't tell me what happened, other than to mutter about him thinking he could do an interstate booty call. Whatever happened, I can tell she's crushed, but she will not admit it.

I call Kendra that day and tell her about seeing Danielle on TV.

"You gotta be happy for her," she says.

"I know."

"But it's OK to still be sad for you."

"I knew you would understand," I say.

"At least you know now. And it doesn't mean you'll never see each other again."

Then she tells me her news. She and her mom should be getting their housing on the base in Bellvoir around the beginning of March.

"That's great!"

"Yeah, but I felt kind of bad telling you," she says. "I know how much you want to go back. And Bellvoir isn't really *home* home."

"Don't feel bad. When we get the trailer, we'll be close enough."

When I tell her about Tru disappearing, she says, "Don't worry. Come on, you two ended up at the same school together after meeting in the back bayou. How much more meant-to-be-together do you want? He's probably going to show up singing under your window. Go look. He's probably out there right now!"

It's silly, but I do it. He's not there.

I try Hip again the next day. I get his voice mail. "Hi, Hip. Hope you had a great holiday. Just wanted to check in about Tru. To see if you heard anything from your relatives?" I try again the following day but don't leave a message. On New Year's Eve, I try one more time and he picks up. "Hi, it's Evangeline Riley. Sorry. Just. Any news on Tru?"

He definitely sounds like he was hoping it was someone else. "I haven't heard anything, but you know who might know? Kaye Pham. Do you know her? She's in Baton Rouge. They were, um, friends. Do you want her number?"

I would rather die than call Kaye Pham to ask her where Tru is. "Sure," I say. And I write down the number, knowing I will never call it and can't call Hip back again, either, because he's basically telling me not to call him again.

"Thanks," I say. "Are you going back to Bayou Perdu?"

"I don't think so," he says. "We're going to try to get a boat in Galveston Bay somewhere."

"OK. Well, thanks for trying to help me. Happy New Year."

"Sorry I wasn't much help," he says. "Tru's a good guy. He's one of my favorite cousins. I'd really like to hear from him, too. If you hear, tell him to give me a call."

"Will do," I say, my throat closing up.

I spend New Year's Eve at Chase's house, with his parents and their rich friends, Sophie, Claire, and Derek, who once again steals the show with his trombone. All the talk swirling around me: New Year's resolutions, people starting the year strong, starting over. The only things I want are to get back home and to get back to Tru. People say you've got to really go for what you want. So the only thing I can think is that I have to call Kaye.

I wait until the day after New Year's Day because I imagine her sitting around watching football with her family on New Year's and, really, I would rather do anything in the world than make this call. But the next day, around lunch, I do it, desperate for her to not pick up, but desperate for her to tell me, yes, she has seen Tru and she will give him my number.

She picks up on the second ring. "Hello?"

"Hi, is this Kaye?"

"Yes?"

My heart is pounding. "Hi, Kaye. This is Evangeline Riley. From Bayou Perdu?"

"Oh, hey!" She sounds confused but not unhappy to hear from me.

"Hey! I got your number from Hip Tran. He said that you were in Baton Rouge now."

"Yeah, since Katrina."

"Is all your family OK?"

We have a few exchanges about what happened to us and about people we know and where they are now. "So are you living in Houston? Near Hip?" she asks.

"Atlanta, actually. Hip is a friend of my sister's boyfriend. He thought you might be able to help me." In a split second, I decide to lie. "I was the manager for this band here in Atlanta. And one of our members had to leave suddenly and we think he went to Baton Rouge and we need to get in touch with him. His name is Tru Nguyen—do you know him?"

Silence. Too long a pause. Then stammering. "Uh, yeah, I know him. But I haven't seen him since before Katrina. He's . . . he's in Baton Rouge?" She sounds really surprised.

"That's what we think. For a few weeks." This is awkward beyond belief. "Hip thought, I guess, that you might know where he is."

"Uh. No, I didn't know he was here. I haven't seen him."

"Oh. OK. Well, listen. If you do see him, could I get you to ask him if he could call?"

"Uh, sure," says Kaye. "Hold on. Let me get a pen."

"Thanks, Kaye. We really need to get in touch with him." Somehow I just can't say *I.*

"Sure, no problem. If I see him."

When I hang up, I feel relief wash over me. Surely this will work. Surely I will reach him.

Holding Pattern

WHEN AN UNFAMILIAR NUMBER shows up on the phone a few days later, I hesitate for a moment. There are two people it might be, two people who I really want to talk to. Or maybe it's just a wrong number. I let it ring three times, bracing myself for disappointment. But when I say hello, it's a familiar voice I hear. It's Danielle.

"Evangeline?"

"Danielle? Oh, my God, is it really you?"

In one split second, that shadowy figure, that ghost of my best friend that's been haunting me for months, becomes solid: a voice coming through the speaker. I feel this rush of pure joy.

"It's me," she says. "That stupid producer lady gave me your number. I can't believe that's the thing that would get us back in touch. I guess you saw the show. So embarrassing. They made me look like such a dork."

"No, you looked good. You looked great."

"No, really, I didn't." There's a nervousness in her voice. The kind I used to notice when she talked to strangers, not to me.

"So . . ." I pause. Where do we begin? I know part of her story—what I saw on the show at least—but she doesn't know any of mine. "Where . . . ?" I start to ask where she is right now because I think maybe we can go backward from there, but she talks over me, asking, "Are you at your aunt's house? Oh, wait, were you going to say something?" We talk over each other again.

"You go first," she says.

I try to tell her in our own familiar way—fast and full of sarcasm and a little bit of drama. But it feels like it's falling flat. There's a silence when there should be an "Oh, my God!" Or her laughter is off just a beat. But when we get to the part about me having to call Kaye Pham, that's when we have a breakthrough.

"Oh, God, noooooo!" she squeals. "That's the worst!"

"I knew you'd understand."

We start talking about people from home. She hasn't

heard anything about anyone, so I tell her what I know and I can tell she is eager to hear it.

"So Bayou Perdu High is just not going to reopen? Everyone's going to Bellvoir now? What are you going to do?"

"We're going back when we get our trailer. Well, at least that's what I want. Mama said she's never going back, but I don't believe her."

"That doesn't sound like her. I mean your mom is, like, *the queen* of Bayou Perdu."

"There's not really anything to be the queen of now."

We talk about the people who we know are going back — April Dubcheck and Kendra. "So," says Danielle, her tone changing, "I guess you heard on the show that *we're* not coming back. Especially now. Desiree is pregnant. She and Alan are getting married on Valentine's Day."

"Oh, my God."

"Alan's great. Really. But don't be fooled by the happy ending they gave us in the documentary. She's still putting the man in her life above me, even if he is a good one. And now the new baby. I'm lonely a lot. I miss you."

Her words drop into me, a lead sinker on the end of a long line. "I miss you, too."

We promise we will keep in touch, now that we can. I ask her for her mailing address so I can send her the scarf I made with the yarn she gave me for my birthday.

Later, I ride to the grocery store with Daddy and I tell

181

him about my call with Danielle. "We were talking about who has gone back. She was asking when we were."

He stares straight ahead, never taking his eyes off the road. "Let's not get ahead of ourselves."

"But when the trailer . . ."

"There's no point in talking about that now. You just concentrate on doing well in school. We'll cross that bridge when we come to it."

And the conversation is over.

Danielle and I call back and forth a few times with some "I forgot to tell you" bits. But the weird thing is, now that we *can* talk, there isn't that itch. It's not the day-to-day need to tell each other everything like when we were actually together each day. It feels like the closeness we had will really never be the same again.

School starts back and I can't help but compare how different it is to our first day in September. Or maybe it's *us* that's different. Mandy hasn't been hanging out with Lacy lately. She's mostly been home, alone, watching TV or, shockingly, reading books. And me. I'm a different person, too. I was a girl whose life had been destroyed by Katrina. Now I'm just another ordinary teenage girl with family problems and a broken heart.

I see that woman I met on my first day again, that counselor whose name I don't remember.

"Hi, Evangeline!" she says. "I'm Ms. Bell," she adds.

"Oh. Hi," I say.

"You're still here, I see," she says. "How are you settling in to life in Atlanta?"

"Fine," I say.

"Well, remember, if you ever want to talk, my office is just next door to the main office."

"OK," I say, starting to step away.

My new schedule rearranges my life. My lunch isn't at the same time as Chase and Derek's music class, so when I get to the cafeteria the first day back, I look around for a familiar face. When I find one, it's Tate's. He smiles and waves. I wave back. When I get to the end of the lunch line, I see that he's still looking at me. He beckons me to come over. Since I don't have an alternative, I do.

"Hi," he says in his nice and neutral way. "Want to sit with us?"

I look quickly around the table. It's mostly those friends we sat with at homecoming, including that girl who was nice to me, Mary Katherine. I sink into a chair.

"How were your holidays?" Tate asks.

"OK. Fine. Yours?"

"Pretty good. I got a new DS."

I don't even know what a DS is, so I just nod.

"Long time no see," says Mary Katherine. "I've been wondering about you lately. You said you came here from New Orleans, right?"

"Well, close to it . . ."

"My cousin gets to use this condo off Bourbon Street for Mardi Gras, and he invited me and said I could bring friends. You're coming, right, Tate?"

"If my parents let me."

"It'll be interesting to see how Mardi Gras is this year," I say. "If people come back."

"You've been?" asks Mary Katherine.

"Every year."

"You should come with us," she says. "It's a teacher workday on that Friday, so we have it off and we're road-tripping down there."

My mind starts racing. If I could get to New Orleans, surely I could get myself to Baton Rouge from there. Just for a day even. "My parents probably wouldn't let me," I say. "But thanks."

"OK." She shrugs. "But let me know if you change your mind. See you tomorrow!"

It's harder to reestablish the afternoon routine with Chase without Tru. Derek, who now seems to be wildly popular, isn't hanging out with us much. And Chase seems to have developed an interest in Ariel, that girl who was in my political science class. I spend a lot of my time alone, thinking about Tru, imagining when he will call, what our conversation will be like. I keep telling myself I will give Kaye a few weeks before I try her again, but every day seems endless.

Daddy has gone down to Fort Walton, Florida, to do renovations on one of Uncle Jim's rental houses. He's going to be away from the family for a while, but it's good money. Enough to get us through for at least another month. So while he's gone, I babysit a lot so that I'm at least making money. And I spend a lot of time at Aunt Cel's house with Mamere.

"You're hurting, *cherie,*" she says. "A little light has gone out in you."

I nod.

"That young man?"

I nod again. "His family left. I don't know where they went."

She puts her arm around me. "You've been through a lot this year," she says. "More than anyone twice your age should have to go through. But those are the things that make us strong."

I don't want to be strong. I just want to go back to the way it used to be.

The first night Daddy is back from Fort Walton, I sneak into the hall to listen to him and Mama fighting.

"If I can start over here, why can't you?" Mama hisses.

"I've always taken care of this family the best way I can. The best way I can is on the water."

"But it's not enough. It never has been. With my salary,

we can get by if you just keep taking jobs like this. Think about the girls. They're better off here. And so am I."

"Fine," says Daddy. "You and the girls stay here. I'm going back down to finish the job in Fort Walton. And when the trailer comes through, I'm going back alone."

A sick feeling comes over me and I duck back into my room. This can't be happening. He can't mean it. I toss and turn all night, trying to work out how I will talk to him about it, but in the morning when I come down for breakfast, he's already gone.

The next day after babysitting, I go back to Aunt Cel's house. I tell Mamere what I heard the night before.

She sighs. "Darlin', they're both trying to do what's right. None of these decisions are easy."

"But how can *not* going home be right? It's our *home*. Don't you want to go back?" I'm so upset, my voice is trembling.

"With everything the way it is now, it's not my time to go back. I've got something I need to do here and that's be with my Celia. That's the silver lining in this dark storm cloud. And if you look at it, you've got a silver lining, too. It's a good school you're going to. You can learn a lot here. Don't be so set on getting back what you've lost. Think about what you can gain from being here."

Now it feels like even Mamere is against me.

I used to love the feeling I got when I first set out on the water with the horizon line in front of me, knowing that

I could just keep going and going. That feeling of endless possibility. Now when I look into the future, I can only see blankness. There's nothing solid beneath my feet and nothing in front of me. I drift through my days surrounded by a fuzzy sensation, as if all my sharp edges have been worn down.

Mama has drifted off into her new life. She starts talking about going on a "gals' weekend" to the beach with her friends from work, but realizes that it's the week that Aunt Cel is taking Mamere on a cruise, so she seems to put the idea to rest. With Daddy still in Fort Walton, we'd be alone. For some reason, Mandy pushes back.

"Evangeline and I can stay by ourselves, Mama. I'm eighteen!"

This gives Mama pause. I can tell she wants to go on the beach trip. "Well, I guess that's true," she says. "But no one would be allowed in this house."

Mandy rolls her eyes. "Like we know anyone."

"You could call Uncle Jim if something goes wrong. I'll stock the fridge. And I'll be calling to check up on you."

"We'll be fine," says Mandy.

"Why were you so big on getting Mama to leave?" I ask her later when we're in our room.

"What do you mean?" she asks.

"Come on, Mandy. I can tell there's something more to this. You're hiding something."

"Can I trust you?" she asks.

"What do you think?"

She sighs. "OK, Byron and I are trying to get back together. Don't give me that look. Just listen. We've been waiting for a chance to try again. He said he'd come down. If we can just have some time alone together, I think we can work it out. But you have to promise not to breathe a word of this to anyone."

This plan has disaster written all over it. But I agree not to say anything. And then about an hour later, it hits me and I spring up in bed. The weekend she's talking about is the weekend of the Friday teacher workday. The weekend that Mary Katherine and Tate are going to New Orleans. "Mandy. I just thought of a way that you and Byron can have some really, *really* alone time."

"I was thinking," I say to Mary Katherine at school on Monday, "if the offer is still open to come to Mardi Gras, I would love to go with you. See, the thing is . . . I have this friend in Baton Rouge I need to see, and if I could just get as far as New Orleans with you, I can take it from there. I'll pay you for gas."

"Awesome!" says Mary Katherine. "But you're welcome to stay with us as long as you want."

"Maybe the first night?" I'm trying to think this through. If we get there late Friday and I take a bus up to Baton Rouge the next morning, it could work. But even though I run through every option, I always end up in the same place. I need to know more about where Tru is, and I can't do that without calling Kaye again. I just have to. But it takes me a few days before I can work up my courage to do it.

"Hey, Kaye, it's Evangeline Riley again!" I try to sound perky but rushed, so she knows I won't keep her on the phone long.

"Hi," she says, sounding less than thrilled to hear from me.

"Listen, just one quick thing. I'm getting a ride down to New Orleans the weekend before Mardi Gras with some friends. And I was thinking of coming up to Baton Rouge . . ." Now I start grasping around wildly for a reason she needs to help me find Tru. "Remember I told you I was looking for Tru Nguyen, who was in that band I managed? Well, I wondered if you'd seen him yet. Because I have this check I need to drop off for him. From this show they played. And I know he could really use the money." I'm pleased with myself for coming up with such a convincing lie.

Silence. "Well, I think I saw his sister at the Vietnamese Community Center. If you went there, someone could probably give him the check," she says finally.

"Oh, gosh, that's great, Kaye, thank you so much!" I'm feeling incredibly grateful to her. "I'd love to see you when I come up," I add.

"Um, OK," she says.

"Well, I'm going to be getting there sometime in the late morning on the Saturday before Mardi Gras." I'm completely making this up. "So could I call you when I arrive at the bus station in Baton Rouge? I mean, I hate to ask, but I don't know where the community center is or if there's a city bus to get there. Do you have a car? Maybe you could meet me at the bus?" I'm pushing it.

"Um, sure," she says. "I guess just call me the day before and let me know when you're getting there." She sounds like she is agreeing to go have her teeth pulled. But *she said yes*. So I'm going with that.

"Oh, Kaye. You are the *best*. Thank you so much!"

So that's it. A car is leaving from my school for New Orleans on Friday morning. I am going to be in it.

Mama takes off for her girls' getaway Friday morning. I meet Tate, Mary Katherine, and their friends — Bailey, Brent, and Lee — in the parking lot at school, and we pile into Mary Katherine's mom's minivan.

During one of our rest stops on the way down, I walk away from the group and call Kaye. I get her voice mail. "Hi, Kaye, this is Evangeline. I'm on my way down to New Orleans. Just call me so we can arrange a ride tomorrow to the Vietnamese Community Center. I so appreciate your help. Thanks!"

After what seems like the longest trip back down to

Louisiana ever, we're finally crossing over the causeway. I get some kind of invisible infusion—I feel strength, the strength of home flooding into me.

"Wow."

"Oh, my God, look at that."

Everyone else in the car is pointing out horrors of the destroyed buildings as we drive through New Orleans East.

For me, this beautiful, desolate, almost unrecognizable place is still home.

We exit into the Quarter and find a place to park. The wet Louisiana air hits me the second I open the door, and I suck it in like I've been holding my breath for months. *Home. Home.* Everything feels like it's coming together. Tomorrow I might see Tru. So tonight while I'm here, I might as well have fun.

Passing through the crowds on the way to the condo, I'm struck by the music and color, the atmosphere. Maybe there aren't as many people here this Mardi Gras, but those who did make it are partying twice as hard to make up for it. A couple of topless women come up and hug Tate, exclaiming, "You're adorable! Isn't he adorable?" He turns beet red. Three people dressed as gnomes in red pointed hats and blue tops approach. "There's no place like gnome!" one says, and hands us all a pile of beads.

There are police and National Guardsmen all over the place. I guess they're afraid of looting. But so far it's just a bunch of rowdy drunks.

There are dozens of people at the condo when we get there. Bailey asks where we are going to sleep, and some guy says, "Oh, don't plan on getting any sleep tonight!" I think we are expected to crash on the floor since the college kids already have the bedrooms. "We'll figure it out later," says Mary Katherine. "Let's go out and explore."

Her cousin Brice starts to list the places that are lax about IDs. One of them I remember Mandy has gone to, so I suggest that one. The college friends of Brice's are staying in for a while, so they lend their fake IDs to everyone who needs them, which of course includes me. Apparently my name is Grace and I'm from Smyrna, Georgia. The picture doesn't really look like me at all, but I know they won't be picky.

I nervously pass the bouncer, who gives a skeptical glance at all the IDs but lets us in anyway. The bar is full of tourists, mostly kids like us. It's loud and people are already drunk even though it's only around five o'clock. We go out to the courtyard.

"Can I get you a drink?" Tate asks. "Hurricanes for everyone?"

"I'll just have a sip of yours," I say. "They're really strong, you know."

Mary Katherine and I perch on the edge of a big planter since there's nowhere to sit.

"This is so cool!" she exclaims. "I can't believe we're in New Orleans. And you lived here?"

"Not exactly," I explain. "About forty-five minutes from here. It's really different."

"You must miss it," she says.

"All the time."

"So, are you going there tomorrow?"

"No, it's Baton Rouge I'm going to," I say. "To see . . . my boyfriend, actually."

"I knew it!" she exclaims. "Tell me about him."

I find myself opening up to her. I'm going to see him tomorrow. It's really going to happen.

"What about you?" I ask her. "Is there someone in your life?"

She gets kind of a secret smile on her face. "Well, not yet. But there is someone I've had my eye on for a while. And I think things might be *very* close to changing for us."

When Tate comes back with the drinks, somehow I end up having more than just a sip.

He goes back for a second round, and I have a moment of pause. Two Hurricanes isn't a good idea for anyone. But everyone's having such a good time. It seems a shame to be the voice of reason. I tell him to get me one. I check my phone again. Nothing from Kaye yet.

Mary Katherine gets a message from Brice to come back so they can have the IDs because they want to go out, and everyone sucks down their drinks really quickly. "Oooh, brain freeze!" says Tate.

We get back to the condo and there's loud music playing

and the balcony windows are open with people hanging off, throwing beads onto the street. There are empty beer cans *everywhere*. Tate heads into the kitchen, then comes back with two beers, offering me one. "No, thanks," I say.

He pops the top and has a sip, then grimaces. "Eww, you're right. It's awful. I wonder if they have anything else." As it turns out, someone has lined a plastic garbage pail with a bag and filled it with some kind of alcoholic punch, and people are just scooping it into plastic cups. I have a feeling this might end up being kind of a wild night. I glance down at my phone. Still no word from Kaye.

It's not even eight o'clock yet and everyone is really drunk.

Mary Katherine, who has been throwing beads from the balcony, comes in and gives me a big hug.

"You are so sweet," she says. "We should hang out more."

The music is loud. It's impossible to have a conversation, so I nod.

"I really feel like I can trust you. So I'm going to tell you a secret. But first I'm going to get more of that yummy punch."

When she stumbles off, I glance down at my phone. Finally. There's a text. My heart skips a beat. I step into the empty bedroom to check it.

This is Elly Reynolds. Kaye is too nice to say it but will you please STOP harassing her? She was dating Tru before Katrina and now they're getting back together. It is RUDE for you to keep trying to contact him through her. BACK OFF.

I've read in books or heard in songs people describing the moment when they feel their hearts break. I never really understood it. But now I physically feel something *break* inside me. There is a weight pressing hard on my chest. I slide down the wall I've been leaning against. This whole time, it never entered my mind that he wasn't out there feeling the same way I did—longing for me the way I was longing for him. How could I have been so stupid? This whole time, it's been over and I didn't even know it.

The door opens and Tate comes in. "Oh there you are," he slurs. He must see something in my face because he comes over and sits next to me on the floor. "Are you OK?"

I can't even fake it. I shake my head. "Bad news. From that friend I was going to see tomorrow." It comes out like a whisper.

"Oh, I'm sorry," he says. He puts his hand on my knee. I can smell sticky-sweet alcohol on his breath. "Is there something I can do?"

I shake my head.

"Because," he starts, and I feel a shift. The walls start to close in, the space shrinks. It's just me, him, and my sadness all together in this dark room away from the loud music and craziness on the other side of the door. "I would really do anything for you. Ever since we met. I just think you're really amazing."

195

I look up and into his eyes. They are full of *longing*. And before I know it, I close my eyes and I am kissing him. I am kissing him hard, pressing into his lips like I want them to hold me up, kissing, kissing, searching for something, something I had with Tru and not finding it. I stop kissing him and open my eyes. His eyes are closed. He opens them and gets this sleepy smile that makes me feel completely disgusted with myself. Then his expression changes. "Wow," he says. "That was — wow. Can you excuse me for a second, though?" He gets up a little shakily. The door to the room's bathroom is open a crack and he stumbles toward it. But he doesn't make it. He leans over and starts hurling, loudly.

"Oh, God!" I scramble to my feet. He is doubled over on the floor, with bright-red vomit coming out of his mouth. "Let me get you some water."

I yank open the door and reenter the noise and light and craziness. I rush into the kitchen, brushing past a bunch of people, and fill a plastic cup with water, then grab some paper towels before starting back to the bedroom, where I run into Mary Katherine. "What's wrong?" she asks.

"Tate's sick."

She follows me back into the bedroom where Tate's still on his knees, kind of groaning. The smell is awful. I start cleaning up, but I need more paper towels and finally just go into the bathroom to get a towel to mop up the puke. Mary Katherine is helping him up and getting him into bed. I take the vomity towel and try to clean it off in the shower. When

I come back, Mary Katherine is tipping water up to Tate's mouth. I take his shoes off and get him under the comforter. I pull the trash can next to the bed in case he pukes again, which seems likely. She gets into the bed on the other side of him. "Could you get him a wet washcloth for his forehead?" she asks.

There's nothing in the bathroom that passes as a washcloth, so I get another towel and wet the edge of it. "It's OK," she says to him, dabbing his forehead with the wet cloth. "You just sleep. I'm going to be right here for you."

Suddenly I realize it's *him*. He's the special someone she's been longing for. There's only one thought in my head. *I need to get out of here.*

"I think I'm just going to go out and get a little air," I say to Mary Katherine.

"It's OK. I'll take care of him," she says.

I gather my things. I know I'm not coming back.

I walk toward the river, *my* river, making my way through the revelers, the joyful music issuing out of the open doors of the bars. I feel the bracing wind off the river and see the barges — the same barges that would pass us by in Bayou Perdu. There is only one phrase repeating again and again in my brain: *you are such a fool.*

We felt so big to me. So solid. So real. But what did I really know about Tru? We had a few months together — that's all. Everything I thought I knew was a lie.

When I get to the riverfront, I just sit there and stare

197

out over the water. Empty and numb. Couldn't I just get on one of those barges and go away? And when it passed Bayou Perdu, I could hop off onto the levee and be home. Start over again. Pretend none of this ever happened. I could pick up the pieces of myself and put them back together again. But everything is broken. My family, my friends—everything. I feel like the fight has gone out of me.

After a while, I start walking back to the Quarter. It's chaotic here. It's getting cold. And I don't know where I'm going to sleep tonight.

If it were a few weeks from now, Kendra and her mom would be back on base and I could call them and they'd come pick me up. They'd be here in half an hour. But they're not back yet. No one is back yet.

Just as I'm thinking this, I pass the French Quarter praline store and it hits me all at once. The box of pralines we get every Christmas from Delbert, Mrs. Menil's big-time lawyer son. *I hope I can find some way to return all the favors you did for Mama and me,* he wrote on his Christmas card this year.

Delbert lived in the house next door to Mamere and Grandpere his whole childhood. He was in the grade between Mama and Aunt Cel in school, but they were never close. Mama always makes comments like "Well, you know, Delbert was always good at *decorating*" without coming right out and saying he is gay. Boys like Delbert get out of Bayou Perdu, head straight for New Orleans, and never come back, and that's pretty much what Delbert did, except he would come back regularly to visit his mama. But the day-to-day stuff fell to us—things like opening the lid of the unopenable pickle jar, climbing a ladder and getting something off the roof, fixing the clogged-up toilet for her. But I have found a way that he can return the favor.

I call information for the number, and it's there: D. Menil on Octavia Street. I dial.

"Hello?" There is music in the background. Loud music. People talking.

"Delbert?"

"Yes?"

"This is Evangeline Riley."

Pause. "Oh, hey, dawlin'! How you been?"

"OK. I'm in New Orleans."

"Oh, that's great. But listen, sugar, I'm havin' a party tonight. Mama and I would love to see you, though. We've got the Krewe of Freret parade in the mornin', but we'll be here tomorrow late afternoon if y'all want to stop by. Is your whole family with you?"

I take a deep breath. "Delbert. I'm by myself in the Quarter. I need a place to stay tonight."

"Good Lord, child!" he shouts. "Get yourself on a street-car and come up here. Do you have enough for the fare?"

"Yes."

"Get off at Jefferson. I'm two blocks down on Octavia, on the left. We'll expect you within the hour."

I make my way through the crowds with my head down, then get on the streetcar, which is filled with the usual assortment of Mardi Gras drunks. There are no seats available, so I stand holding a strap the whole way, listening to the conversation of the couple sitting below me.

"Pee-cahn or pee-can?" the man, wearing a giant floppy jester hat, slurs to the woman, who is dressed as some sort of Greek goddess.

"Pee-can," she says.

"You sure about that?" He taps the person sitting next to him on the back. "'Scuse me, sir. How do you pronounce the word spelled P-E-C-A-N?"

The man, who's in a uniform and appears to be coming home from his shift at a hotel, doesn't seem to have any use for this nonsense. "Pee-can," he says gruffly.

"Told you," says the goddess.

I can feel him looking at me. "Hey, miss, miss." He tugs on my jacket. "Pee-cahn or pee-can?"

"Pee-cahn," I say.

"See?" he gloats to the woman.

It's strange that the farther uptown we go, the less it seems like Katrina ever happened. Every once in a while there's a blue tarp over a roof, but those big houses on St. Charles look as perfect and untouchable as they ever did.

I get off at Delbert's stop and head down the dark, quiet street. It's a beautiful neighborhood. The gaslights flicker on the front porches and a few houses are lit up, but as I get closer, I can tell there is a party going on ahead in one of the graceful old homes. It's not quite a mansion, but has those white columns on the front porch, so it looks impressive. There's music drifting out the windows—something old-fashioned and jazzy. The people spilling onto the lawn are wearing costumes, really amazing ones that did not come from the Dollar Store. As I approach the house, someone starts toward me dressed as Glinda the Good Witch from *The Wizard of Oz*—I can tell by the distinctive crown. Then I realize it's Delbert. I've only ever seen him in khakis and a button-down.

"Oh, thank heavens you made it," he says, giving me a hug. My whole body relaxes somehow. He's from home. And Glinda and those gnomes were right: *There's no place like home.*

"Come on in, girl. Let's get you a drink. Nonalcoholic, of course," he says with a wink. "Unless you want one. How old are you now?"

"Sixteen."

"Oh, well, forget it then, honey."

Inside, people are milling around Delbert's elegant living room, with high ceilings and decorative plasterwork. They have champagne glasses, and the music is loud but sophisticated. It's like a movie. Delbert gets me a ginger ale and shows me upstairs to a guest room where I can "put my things," which would be my backpack. "You can stay here tonight, sugar," he says. "No questions asked. We'll talk about it tomorrow. Come down and see Mama now."

Mrs. Menil is on the back veranda, enthroned in a big wicker chair, dressed as a cat. She's got face paint and a headband with little furry ears, and she's wearing a fluffy jacket of some type. When she sees me, she breaks into a big smile. "Dawlin'! You come here and give me a hug." I don't think she's ever hugged me in her life.

It turns out that Katrina was good for Mrs. Menil. Delbert goes to dinner parties all the time and always brings her along. His friends all call her Mama. "I should have moved up here years ago!" she says. She is jolly—laughing and making jokes. I've never seen her happier.

Later, when I'm in the coziest bed I've ever been in, I can hear the sounds of the party drifting lightly through the walls. But otherwise I am alone with the realization that I got it all wrong. I've always trusted my gut, like Daddy has always told me to do. *It'll never steer you wrong,* he says. But it was dead wrong this time. I guess I really don't know anything about love.

In the morning, there are party guests still there, some still wearing portions of their costumes or makeup that's now smeared on their faces. Mrs. Menil seems not to have made it down yet. Delbert is no longer Glinda; he's his usual preppy self, with a clean, pressed shirt, making what he calls his "hangover cure" breakfast for everyone: fried eggs with some Tabasco on the side, a bowl of cheese grits. I sit down at the table, which is set with beautiful silverware and plates, and a good-looking, younger guy pours me some orange juice from a glass pitcher. "So," he says, sliding into the chair next to me. "What's your story?"

"Evangeline's mother grew up in the house next door to me, Jason," says Delbert as he fries bacon. "Her family's been looking in on Mama for years. Her daddy cuts the grass for her and fixes her fence and all kinds of things. They've been very good to us. They're up in Atlanta since Katrina."

"You down for Mardi Gras?" Jason asks.

"Not exactly," I say. And then it's as if I turn off my discretion switch. I start telling this whole room full of strangers what happened.

"Oh, girl . . ." starts the guy in last night's blue eye shadow and mascara. "Drama-rama."

I tell them the part about Elly's text.

"Elly Reynolds. What a bitch!" says the mascara guy. "Tell her to mind her own beeswax."

"Here, let me see the text," says Jason.

I hand him my phone.

"Look," says Jason. "She says they're *getting* back together. Not that they're actually together. Circumstantial evidence."

"I think you mean hearsay," says Delbert.

"Yeah, hearsay. Why take her word for it?" says Mascara Guy. "She's obviously trying to make trouble. You text her

203

right back and tell her to get her nose out of your business. Here, let me do it — I'll set her straight."

I'm slightly terrified that he will, but Jason rolls his eyes and hands the phone back to me. "Elly Reynolds is definitely meddling. Take what she says with a grain of salt."

They are making me feel better.

"But I made it worse," I say. "I was with these friends. This guy friend. And he was drunk and he kissed me and I kissed him back. And then he threw up."

The room explodes in laughter, but it's a sympathetic laughter.

"I've been there, sister," says Mascara Guy.

"If I had a dime for every guy who threw up after he kissed me, I'd be living on my yacht in the Caribbean," says a guy with a do-rag on his head.

"I feel like throwing up just *thinking* about kissing you," Jason jokes, and they make faces at each other.

I explain how embarrassed I am, how awful it will be going back there and facing Tate. And what if he told Mary Katherine, who likes him, that we kissed?

"Oh, honey, don't even think about it. Stay here. I'm going to get you on a plane home tomorrow," says Delbert.

My jaw literally drops. "Oh, no. I mean, thank you. I couldn't, though."

"I won't hear another word about it," says Delbert. "It's the least I can do."

I've never been on a plane before. How much must it cost?

"Just stay here and have fun with us," says Jason brightly. "We'll show you a good time. I don't drink, either. Not like these degenerates," he adds with a wink, looking around at the other guests.

I send a text to Tate: *Hope you're feeling better. I'm with my next-door neighbor from home. I'm going to stay here and they'll get me back to Atlanta tomorrow. Thanks and have fun!* I get a text back from him around three: *Sorry about last night. I don't really remember much. See you at school.*

So I go to Krewe of Freret and spend the weekend with five middle-aged gay men and an eighty-year-old woman. It is the best place that I could be. They're my people. I can just be Bayou Perdu Evangeline here.

When Delbert and I have a moment alone together, I bring up the plane ticket. "I really appreciate your offer for the ticket. And right now I don't know what else I would do. But I have to pay you back for it. I babysit after school a lot. It might take a few months, but I will pay you back."

"Listen," he says. "It's not open to discussion. I'm giving this to you. It's a gift. Everyone gets into spots like this when they're around your age. I know I did. And someone bailed me out. I'm paying it forward. When you can, you'll help out someone younger who needs it, too. And besides, you and your family are good neighbors, and good neighbors help each other out."

I tell him about my parents' plan: Daddy coming back, the rest of us staying in Atlanta.

"How do you feel about that?" he asks.

"All I want to do is get back to Bayou Perdu," I say.

"That's funny," he says. "All I wanted to do when I was your age was get *away* from it." He looks like he's thinking hard about something. "I'm going to tell you something, and I hope I'm not overstepping my boundaries. You are at an important point in your life, where you can start making decisions for yourself. They're not always going to be the right ones. But they need to be *yours*. It's not easy to go against what your parents think is right. Trust me—I know that. But at the end of the day, you have to be true to yourself, whatever that may be."

He puts me in the cab to the airport on Sunday morning with a printout of the ticket he bought me and a ten-dollar bill to give the cabdriver as a tip.

"And a bit more unsolicited advice," he says. "Don't lose your head over some guy. If it's meant to be, it'll be."

When I get home that afternoon after the plane, train, and bus, Mandy is alone, watching TV. There's something subdued about her.

"How'd it go with Byron?"

She shakes her head. "I ended it," she says with genuine

sadness. "The thing with me and Byron is, we have so much history together. And I guess I kind of realized that's all we've got. You can't mistake history for a future."

"I'm sorry," I say. "But I think you made the right decision."

"What about you?" She's sympathetic when I tell her. "Don't believe Elly Reynolds," she says.

"But what else do I have to go on? He hasn't been in touch in over two months." That's a hard fact, not just hearsay, like Jason said.

On Monday, I see Mary Katherine in the hall. I'm terrified that she knows I kissed Tate, but to my shock, she comes rushing over with a smile on her face. "Oh, I'm so glad you made it back!" she chirps. "I got your message about not needing a ride because your neighbor got you a plane ticket. Awesome!"

"How did it go for the rest of the trip?"

She is beaming. "Uh-mazing. You know after you helped me with Tate, I just stayed by his side all night. And by the end of the weekend, we were really together!"

I feel myself blushing. "That's great, congratulations!"

"How'd it go with your boyfriend in Baton Rouge?" she asks enthusiastically.

"We're not together anymore," I say.

Her face falls. "I'm so sorry," she says. "His loss."

When I see Tate at lunch, it's clear that he doesn't remember the kiss at all.

"Well, did you have your long-awaited reunion?" Chase asks when I see him after school.

I tell him what happened. His mouth drops.

"That doesn't sound right," he says, shaking his head. "I don't think you should just take that girl's word for it. Also, I think you should start bombarding her phone with hate messages. Really make life hell for her."

"Not my style," I say.

"Totally my style," he says. "Give me her number."

Instead we go to the taqueria for chips, and we spend hours concocting fake revenge strategies to exact on Kaye and Elly. "I mean it, though," says Chase when he's dropping me off at home. "Tru just isn't the kind of guy who would do that."

The shock of that weekend has turned into numbness, and now the numbness has just settled on me, like a fine coat of dust. It prevents me from feeling most anything. Some days it's all I can do to get out of bed in the morning and drift through my day. Sometimes I think I should call Danielle and share it with her. But who wants to talk when all you've got to share is bad news?

About a week later, I get a note from the office. It's a request that I report to the counselor. I can feel heat rising up my neck. What did I do?

The sign on the office door says MS. BELL, GUIDANCE. Maybe it's about college applications. I knock.

"Come in." Her voice is friendly, warm.

I push the door open.

"Hi, Evangeline. How are you?" she asks, as if we've known each other forever.

"Fine."

"I'm sure you're wondering why I asked you here today."

I nod.

She glances down at a file open on her desk. I recognize my handwriting.

"You were displaced by Hurricane Katrina last fall. That must be tough." She's scanning my face. "That's a lot to go through." She sounds sincere. But I can't make myself say a word.

"Do you know anyone here in Atlanta?" she asks.

"My aunt. My grandmother came with us."

"It's great to have that support."

I nod. She keeps looking right at me with this sympathetic look.

"Evangeline, have you seen a counselor or a therapist since Katrina?"

I shake my head. I didn't know anyone who'd seen a therapist until Chase told me his parents made him go to one when he got kicked out of the conservatory.

"The teachers and I work together to identify students who might need help and probably wouldn't ask for it." She lifts the paper on her desk. Of course, it's one of my personal experience essays from English class. I knew I shouldn't have turned that in. "Ms. Fine was concerned after she read your essay that you might be experiencing depression as a result of your displacement." She glances down at the page again. "You're an amazing writer. The images that you talk about seeing after Katrina. I can't imagine having to go through that. What you're describing here—the numbness, not being able to sleep. Those are symptoms of depression. It's not uncommon in teenagers in general, but also for people who've undergone the kind of trauma you've experienced."

I feel this strange floating sensation, like I'm above this scene looking down at it.

"Writing it out—as you did here in this essay—is one way to work through things. But talking could help, too. You can come talk to me anytime. You don't have to have an appointment. Just stop by." She hands me a brochure. *Depression: What It Is and What You Can Do About It.* The girl in the black-and-white picture has a faraway look in her eyes and is staring off into the distance.

Sitting in the back of Precalculus, I take out the brochure.

It's the feeling I get. I feel it now, but it's different— fear mingled with relief. I'm afraid that I have something. Something that has a name. That feeling of going around like I'm touching everything through heavy gloves, hearing sounds muffled through a thick layer of fluff, vague and indistinct. I slip the brochure back into my notebook.

The next day after lunch, I stop by Ms. Bell's office. She's sitting with her back to the door and I almost walk away. But just as I'm about to, she turns and notices me. Her face lights up.

"Hi, Evangeline! It's great to see you back here. Come on in." She ushers me to a chair.

Honestly, I don't know what I'm doing here. "I read the brochure," I say.

She nods again and looks as if she's waiting for me to say something. "Is there . . . I mean, is it something you have to take medication for?"

"Not necessarily. For some people, medication is the answer. For others, just talking to someone can help."

So I start talking to Ms. Bell. She listens to everything I say about my family, nodding, sometimes saying only "Hmmm" or "How did you feel about that?" I find that the fact that she doesn't talk makes me want to talk more. I tell her things that don't seem important, and sometimes she'll ask me a question about them and then I'll realize that maybe they are. Like the way Mandy and I have always fought. She'll say things like "Sounds like you two are really different" or "Sounds like you've formed some alliances in your family." I thought that I would be talking about Tru. But what comes out is about my family. "Sounds like you're often in the role of helper," Ms. Bell says one day. "But you could use some help, too, sometimes. It's OK to ask for help. It's OK to need things from other people."

I tell her about Danielle. How close we were. How I thought that when we finally reconnected, we'd be talking all the time. But it hasn't turned out that way. Once we caught up on everything that happened to us, it was obvious that things couldn't be the same. We were living different lives. And one of the big reasons we'd been so close before was that we'd been so close physically.

"I always thought that our friendship was more than that. I never thought it would depend on being in the same place."

"It sounds like it *is* deeper than that. You can still cherish her friendship the way you always have, but the way you *maintain* your friendship will be different. It's painful to make these changes, no doubt about it. But you can always hold a place in your heart for her."

We talk about my wanting to go home.

"It's completely natural for you to feel that way," she says. "It's home."

"And I want to help fix it."

"Of course you do," she says. "It's the place you love."

I don't know how it works, but when I leave her office, I feel lighter somehow. Something has lifted.

I think about suggesting to Mandy that she talk to Ms. Bell too, but I know better than that. I don't think talking is what she needs. She needs to hit a softball really hard. She needs to run fast and feel the wind behind her. She needs to win.

"You know varsity softball tryouts are next week, right?" I ask her one night when we are doing our homework at that tiny kitchen-bar countertop before I go visit Mamere.

She looks up at me suspiciously. "Why? Are you thinking of trying out?"

I roll my eyes. "Come on. Why wouldn't you do it? When Byron was here over Christmas, you said you would."

She shakes her head. "I'm *never* going to humiliate myself again after what happened with cheerleading." It strikes me how she sounds just like Mama. *I'm NEVER coming back here.*

"You are one of the best players in the entire state of Louisiana. Why wouldn't you make the team?"

She gets up and walks away.

She needs my help. "I could catch if you want to practice."

She sighs and comes back to the counter, her shoulders slumped. She looks me in the eye.

"I don't know. I might."

I notice when I come back from Aunt Cel's house that she is in sweatpants, with her hair pulled back in a ponytail. She's humming.

"Been out for a run?" I ask.

She cracks a smile. "Just around the apartment complex. But it feels really good."

When I'm heading to the bus after school a week later, I see a paper taped to the entrance to the gym. It's the names of the people who made the girls' varsity softball team. Mandy's name is on the list. I feel a lift.

And then when I get home, there is even more news.

Daddy is sitting on one of those bar stools at the kitchen counter with a bunch of papers spread out in front of him. I see a big manila envelope sticking over the edge. Everything clenches up in my chest. This is it. It's the paperwork for the trailer.

I am practically standing over him and he still doesn't notice me. I scan the paperwork. It's got an address and a unit number. My heart will beat through my chest. "We got it?" I blurt out.

Daddy looks up. He nods and turns back to the page. I had pictured this differently. That we would be hugging each other, jumping up and down. It's our ticket home. But it hits me hard. Another storm. The storm that will come when I tell them I'm going with him. It feels so much fiercer than Katrina. I put my arm around Daddy's shoulder and he hugs me. We stand there wordlessly for a few long minutes.

I go upstairs and call Kendra. "We got the trailer," I say.

"High five!" Kendra says. "We may beat you back by only a few days!"

"Well, here's the thing. We haven't talked about who's going back yet."

"Oh." She sounds a little less excited now. "Well, keep me posted."

I go downstairs for dinner. Mandy's at softball practice. Daddy's in front of the TV with a bag of chips. Mama says she had a late lunch and she's not hungry. I stand at the refrigerator door and look for something that I can put in the microwave.

I grab a leftover bowl of macaroni and head back upstairs. I'm halfway through my homework when I hear voices raised angrily downstairs.

"So, you're going?" Mama is trying to control her voice so I won't hear.

"I'm going."

"Fine. Go. We'll be in a strange city by ourselves."

"Strange city? You're the one that said this is your *home* now. Your mother and sister are here."

"Oh, please. You're so selfish. Just go. Go and ruin your life. I really don't care anymore."

Silence.

I feel rage welling up in me. Before I know it, I am rocketing down the stairs.

"You think he's selfish? You are the *only* one in this family who doesn't want to go home."

Her face is contorted with shock.

"Evangeline, don't talk to your mother —" Daddy starts.

But I interrupt his interruption. "No, I am not going to shut up. Your stupid friends and your stupid job and your stupid clothes. You could care less what Mandy and I are going through."

"Oh, of course! I'm the bad guy! I caused Hurricane Katrina!" Her face is practically purple now, and her voice is hoarse, cracked. "I worked my fingers to the bone for eighteen years to keep this family afloat. Why is it that you think I want to stay here, Evangeline? Because I'm an evil person? A bad mother? Have you ever thought about the fact that I want more for you? That I want you to have a nice life and a better school and a good place to live so that your life isn't so hard later?"

"I don't care about it being hard. This isn't the life I want."

"Then you're being stubborn and childish. You can't see that you'd be better off here."

I feel something explode in me, like an organ rupturing.

"That's all you care about. Being better off." I wave my hand around wildly. "With the stupid flat-screen TV and the stainless-steel kitchen. What about your family? Why aren't we enough for you?"

The room goes silent. Delbert's words come back to me. *You are at an important point in your life, where you can start making decisions for yourself.*

"*I'm* going back to Bayou Perdu. That's what's best for me. I can either go with Daddy or I'll go back alone and stay with Kendra and Ms. Denise when they get their place. But I *am* going back."

"Don't be ridiculous," Mama says. But I can tell there's a little edge of fear in her voice.

"Evangeline . . ." Daddy starts.

I turn and walk away. I meant every word I said.

Mandy comes in noisily after the lights in the hall have

already been turned off. She bursts into the room in her sweats, her hair in a ponytail, her face beaming. She plops down next to me on the bed.

"Thanks for kicking my butt into trying out for softball. You were right. I am one of the better players. The equipment manager — this guy called Chris — drove me home. First, we stopped to get some water at the gas station, and then he got lost. Then we sat in the car talking for, like, an hour." She finally notices that I'm not responding to her. "What? Why do you look like that?"

"We got our trailer. And I just had a big fight with Mama and Daddy."

I can't read the expression on her face. I know she's wanted to go home as much as I do. Or if not as much, at least somewhere close. But now she looks a little shell-shocked. "Oh." She gets off the bed. "When are we leaving?"

"Not all of us. Only Daddy and me."

She takes off her gym shoes and socks, staring blankly. "You can't leave," she says suddenly. "Please don't leave me."

"What?"

"Evangeline." She looks me straight in the eye with the most frightened expression I think I've ever seen her wear. "I have to tell you something I haven't told anyone." All I can think is *Please don't let her say she's pregnant.*

"I didn't get into LSU. I found out last week."

"Oh, Mandy. I'm sorry. . . ."

"No, you don't understand. I didn't apply anywhere else."

218

"I thought you applied to Lafayette and Monroe."

"I just said I did," she says miserably. "I was sure I'd get into LSU."

It's too late to apply anywhere else now. Mama is going to freak out.

"I don't know what to do. I don't know what's going to happen. Then there's this thing with Chris. . . ." Mandy starts pacing. "Please. Don't leave me here with Mama alone. She's going to kill me."

"Someone needs to stay with Mama."

"Why can't *you* stay?"

"You know I can't. I need to help Daddy."

She glares at me. "That's always the way it is. You and Daddy. You're always on the same team."

"You and Mama are always on the same team."

"I never got to pick. You two always sided against me."

"That's not true."

"I want to go home," says Mandy. "But Chris . . . And now that I don't know what I'm going to do next year . . ." She covers her face with her hands.

"Don't make your decision based on some guy. . . ."

"Really, Evangeline? Unlike you?"

Her words hit me like a punch to the stomach. She's right, of course. "That is not why I want to go back. That's over," I say weakly. "I don't belong here."

"Bloom where you're planted!" Mandy spits at me.

"Like you? Making Ds and getting suspended? Really

blooming, Mandy . . ." Everything is so frustrating. "Look, I'm sorry. But my staying wouldn't help. You're going to have to tell her at some point. We're all basically on our own now. Our family is breaking up."

She plops down on the edge of the bed.

I do the only thing I can think of doing. I reach out and grab her hand, and we sit there like that silently.

The next day, Mama hasn't come downstairs when Mandy and I leave. I can feel Daddy looking at me, but I can't meet his eyes.

After school, Daddy's on the phone with Sheriff Guidry. I slide into the chair near the couch to wait for him to get off.

When he hangs up, he looks at me, holds me in his gaze for a long, uncomfortable minute. "You upset your mother last night."

She upset *me,* I want to say. But I say nothing.

"That diner. She put her heart and soul into it. . . ."

"Are you two getting divorced?"

He sighs. "We're not getting divorced. But we're not going to be together right now. And you wanting to leave . . . it just makes things worse for her."

Something in me turns from determined to desperate. "Daddy . . ." My chin starts to quiver, but I swallow hard. "I need to go home."

The look on his face is tortured. "There's nothing for you there. It's a trailer park. I don't know when I'm going to be able to get back out on the water. I need to find a new boat. Fix it up. All I'm going to be doing is working. You'd be alone and it's not safe. There's no future for you there."

"There's no future for me *here,* Daddy." Part of me feels like I want to fall into his arms crying like I'm ten years old. But honestly, I've never been so sure of anything in my life. "I'm going, Daddy. You can't make me stay."

He shakes his head. It feels so awful to be hurting him like this. But I'm not backing down.

We do our usual Monday at Aunt Cel's. Mamere cooks tasso with red beans and rice. Around the table, there is strained small talk, mostly focused on Mandy's softball team. In fact, Chris is going to pick her up later and we are going to get to meet him. It is a relief to have something to talk about. I haven't spoken a word to Mama since our fight the other night, and as far as I know, she and Daddy haven't spoken, either.

Chris arrives after lunch: blond and gorgeous, of course. He seems brighter than Byron. Then they leave and Aunt Cel takes Mama and Daddy out back to show them her new deck, and I'm alone with Mamere.

"Mamere." I sit down next to her on the sofa, hesitantly. "I'm going back with Daddy."

Her expression is hard to read. "Does he know that?" she asks.

I nod. "They don't want me to. But I'm doing it anyway." It's so hard to be this way with her. I've always been the good girl, the one who does what's she's told.

She stares straight ahead, then reaches out for my hand. "You never did like to take the easy way out," she says finally. "You've always been brave. Ever since you were that tiny child reelin' in a fish that weighed more than you did. You always put your all into it and stuck with it to the end." She turns and looks at me, like she's trying to figure something out. "All these months, all this starting over, you never slipped and fell like your sister did. You kept your chin up and made the best of it. So I know you've thought about it a lot. I know you know your own heart. And if this is what it tells you to do . . ."

It's all I can do not to break down crying. I lean into her, that soft shoulder that's always been there for me. "It is what I want. It's what I have to do. But I don't ever want to leave you. What's going to happen to us?"

"I can't tell you that. The one thing I know about life is that it always moves forward, not backward. The thing is, *cherie*"—she looks me straight in the eye—"things have to break down for the new thing to come in. That's how nature works. The old leaves fall so the new ones can come in. There's a season for everything. We can't stop it, and we shouldn't want to. Are you sure you're looking forward and not back?"

All I know is that when I look into my future, it's not here. It's in the place where I know myself: out there in that limitless place between two skies. Back home.

"I'm sure," I say.

When Mama, Daddy, and Aunt Cel come back inside, Mamere says, "John, Vangie, I need to speak with you. Sit down."

The whole room goes solemn.

Mamere moves to the edge of her seat. "Evangeline has told me that she wants to go back to Bayou Perdu with John."

Mama's face hardens. "Well, I'm not surprised she tried to get you on her side for this," she says. "She's determined to get her way."

"I seem to recall another sixteen-year-old who was determined to get her way despite her parents' wishes," Mamere says.

"I can't believe you would throw that back in my face!" Mama fumes.

"I'm not throwing anything in your face," Mamere says steadily. "Only to remind you that at that age everyone feels ready to make up their own minds. Now, I want us all to talk this out and come to a resolution."

"There's nothing to discuss," says Mama. "It's nearly the end of the school year. She's in a good school with opportunities she'd never have even if she was at Bellvoir High. She wants to go live in a trailer."

"I don't *want* to live in a trailer; it's just what we *have to* do back there." The frustration in me mounts. I close my eyes. This is my only chance to explain it. I take a deep breath and begin again. "You know I've always been the one who helped out, who worked on the boat ever since I was big enough. I don't do it just because I have to. I do it because I love it. Everyone else has always wanted to get out of Bayou Perdu, but I never have. I never wanted to leave, and I still don't. I need it and it needs me. Not later, but now. There's nothing here for me—I am sure of that. I need to go back. I *am* going back."

The silence is awful.

"You know what?" says Mama finally. "I can't talk about this right now. Just go. Go back to Bayou Perdu."

Daddy says nothing. Mamere says nothing.

Mama gets up and puts her purse over her shoulder. "I'm going home." Daddy gets up and follows her. I can't make myself get up off the couch. I look at Mamere. "Can I stay here tonight?"

She nods.

"What did you mean earlier, Mamere?" I muster the courage to ask when we're alone later. "When you said that about another sixteen-year-old being determined to get her way?"

Mamere sighs. "When your mother was sixteen, she was in love with someone who was older than her. He was in the navy. She decided that she was going to marry him no matter what we said about her being too young. She was prepared to leave home and marry him and move onto the base."

I'm confused. "You mean Daddy?"

She shakes her head. "Danielle's daddy. Hank Watts."

Now I'm in shock. "What?"

"You always wondered what your mother had against Desiree. Desiree was a desperate girl who'd had a very unhappy childhood. She swooped in and stole Hank away from your mother in a very deceitful way. So your mother had her reasons for not liking Desiree."

Danielle is the daughter of the man Mama thought she'd marry? "What about Daddy? He was her backup plan?"

"That's not it at all. Your daddy was there for her when she had a broken heart. He has always been there for her. And that's what he's trying to do now, supporting his family the only way he can. She just can't see it that way."

"She can't see *anything* any way but her way."

"You know, when your mama was your age, we didn't always understand each other, either. Even now, we don't. The line between mothers and daughters isn't always easy. Sometimes it skips a generation, like with me and you." She looks at me intensely. "You, I could always understand. We're two peas in a pod." She smiles.

"The only thing I'd stay here for is you," I say.

"*Cherie,* I don't want you doing any such thing on my account," she says. "Your happiness makes me happy. Remember that."

* * *

225

When I see Ms. Bell again, I explain what has happened. "You sound torn about leaving your grandmother," she says.

"I'm afraid if I don't get home now, I'll never get there. But I also don't want to let go."

"Let go of what?"

That's when I finally tell her about Tru.

She asks questions, and I tell her everything. Explain it in a way that sounds new to me. Why he was so important to me. Why he doesn't feel like the past to me, but the future.

"He sounds like a really great guy," says Ms. Bell. "It must have been hard to have him just disappear like that. And the text from your old school friend must have really thrown you. But I wouldn't believe anything until I heard it directly from him. Is there a way you can get in touch?"

I explain how his family couldn't afford a phone for him.

"What about e-mail?" she asks.

We've never had a computer at home. We have a school e-mail address here, but I don't think I've actually checked it. The only people I've ever really wanted to communicate with here are Chase, Tru, and Derek, and I just *saw* them. If Tru had an e-mail address, it would have been cut off because he doesn't go to school here anymore. Still, maybe it's worth checking.

I have to ask the research librarian how to log in because I've forgotten since the orientation last fall. She gets me set up and brings up my in-box. It's full of e-mails. They're all from Tru.

I hold my breath, feel my heartbeat. Close my eyes and open them again. I scroll down. There are dozens of them, starting the week after he left, the first with the subject line *Message in a Bottle*. The latest one was just after Mardi Gras, with the subject *Signing Off.*

I open the first one.

I was trying to think of what you do when you have to get in touch with someone and you don't have a phone or a phone number and you're a million miles away. For some reason, the idea of a message in a bottle came to mind. But you're land-locked, so the next thing that came to mind was e-mail.

I know that you know things weren't going well with my dad's cousin. I guess my dad just didn't like the idea of taking charity, and the truth is, his cousin really was rubbing it in. They would fight about the stupidest little things. I don't even know what it was that set them off, but I could tell there was a lot of tension when I left to go to the show that night. I was waiting for you, and when I didn't see you, I knew something must have happened. I didn't play well. Then my dad showed up and told me we had to go. Right then. When I got to the truck, it was packed, and my mom and sister were inside. That was it. We were leaving. I tried to tell my dad that we couldn't go. I had to say good-bye to you. But I could tell there was no way we were going back.

We are in Baton Rouge with our other cousins now. I started at this new school. I don't even know what to say. I've written a bunch of stuff and erased it again and again. I'm a little lost without you, and that may be an understatement. Remember that song we listened to at Chase's house? I hope that somehow you find this message in a bottle. T

My hands are shaking as I read through, digging out all these precious things he wrote and devouring them like a starving person who has stumbled upon a banquet.

I'm thinking of you. Of course I could have said that at any given moment in the last two weeks. Any given moment since I met you.

Either you're not getting these or don't want to hear from me. I hope it's not that. I guess there is nothing for me to do but keep trying.

I guess I could stop sending these. But it makes me feel like I'm talking to you even if I'm not. There is no one here like you. There's no one anywhere like you.

An ache spreads through me, a loss that's dull in the middle and sharp around the edges. My heart is so heavy.

I can barely contain myself when I read the e-mail from right before Mardi Gras, exactly when I was trying to find him:

I meant to tell you, I saw that girl Kaye from Bayou Perdu. When she came up to talk to me at church, I mentioned you. I said something like "I think you know my girlfriend, Evangeline. She's from Bayou Perdu, too." She got kind of awkward, I guess because of when Hip tried to set us up. Now every time I see her at church, she looks away really quickly. It's weird.

Elly lied. My rage almost boils over. This whole time, the answer that I was dying for was right here. I'm the one who messed everything up.

Signing Off, says the last e-mail.

I'm not going to be able to send these anymore. I have to quit school so I can work full-time to get money for the new boat. You'll probably never get them anyway. I can't say good-bye any better than I could before. I don't ever want to say good-bye to you. But I'm going to find another way to reach you. And hope that when I do, we can start over where we left off. Because I really believe there's supposed to be so much more to us. T

What can I possibly say? If I think about it too long, I may miss another chance. I quickly type out a note, give it the subject line *Coming Home,* and hit send.

I just got your e-mails. I'm so sorry. I didn't check. In case you get a phone, here's my number. We got a trailer and I am going home next weekend. We are going to be together. I'm going to catch up to the things I love. E

* * *

On Friday, I say good-bye to Ms. Bell. She hugs me and gives me a little blank journal with this quote written on the inside cover:

In the middle of winter I at last discovered that there was in me an invincible summer.

—*Camus*

"It reminded me of you, with your hard winter. But I know you have summer inside you. I know it will give you strength," she says.

We hug.

"Keep in touch," she says as she waves good-bye.

It's hard to say good-bye to Chase. "What is it with you people?" he says. "Up and leaving all the time?"

"You're about the only thing I am going to miss here," I say.

"Stop. You know how uncomfortable I am with outward displays of sincere emotion," he says.

"I couldn't have done it without you. Any of it. I mean it. Thank you."

He rolls his eyes. "Just go find your Tru love. You guys are so disgustingly perfect for each other."

"Aww, that's sweet. Thanks."

He says he'll come visit soon. I can't face having him see me in a FEMA trailer. But someday.

I go to Aunt Cel's after school. Aunt Cel invites me to

stay for dinner, packs me a "care package" of things to use when we get to the trailer. I know she doesn't approve of me going, but she's not saying so. When the time comes to say good-bye to Mamere, I feel kind of frozen. It doesn't feel real.

"We've never been this far apart," I say barely aloud as I'm laying my head on her shoulder.

"We're never going to be apart," she says. "Not really. Even when we're not together, we're always a part of each other, *cherie*. I'm a part of you and you're a part of me. Always." She presses an envelope into my hand. It has twenty dollars in it and a bunch of pictures of us together.

"Are you going to come down soon to visit?" I finally choke out.

"I will, *cherie*. I'll be there when it's time."

It's physically hard to let go of her. "Even when we're apart, we're always a part of each other," she repeats. "Remember that. That's the truth."

I wake up early on Saturday. Part of me wants to leave everything here but my purse and the copy of *Evangeline* Mamere gave me. But I pull things out and put them in my backpack. Mandy is still asleep. I go over and sit on the edge of her bed. I shake her a little. She makes a grumpy sound and opens one eye.

"I'm leaving," I say.

She sits up, looking annoyed. Then she does something really unexpected. She puts her arms around me and hugs me tight. A hug with all of her in it—no ego and no posturing. I relax into it, feel some tension go out of me. We hold each other there for what seems like a long time.

"Maybe we'll come down in the summer," she says. "Or maybe you'll come back up."

I nod.

"You get to have your own room in the trailer, at least."

"Good luck with Chris," I say.

"I'll miss you," she says, just loud enough to hear. "Call me a lot."

"I will. I'll miss you, too."

When I go downstairs, Mama is sitting on that big pleather sofa in her bathrobe. She looks old. I sit in the chair opposite her.

She looks at me, but not really. It's like she's looking past me. I think about what Ms. Bell says. That I'm not responsible for other people's feelings. I'm only responsible for my feelings. But right now I feel like a traitor.

Then I can feel her focus on me and I meet her eyes. I can't tell you what passes between us. It's something that feels like shame and sadness. I wish that I could be bigger, could be better, and more forgiving. That I could have softened my position and tried to see her side of things. Maybe she feels that, too.

When I've pictured the gap growing between her and

Daddy in these months, I've always seen it as water. It's flowing in faster and faster and the force of the water erodes any ground they stood on. But between Mama and me, it's like a canyon. A rocky canyon that you'd have to scramble down and up the other side and get all cut up and fall down on the way. I can see her there on the other side, the other side of the room, now. I just can't get there. It's going to take a long, hard descent and a tough climb up the other side.

I hear Daddy come in from the truck. He stands in the doorway. I cross to Mama and we hug, stiffly, wordlessly. I pass Daddy in the doorway, leaving them to say good-bye alone.

When we pass the Atlanta airport, I feel like I've been released from something that had me in its grip. I got away. I'm going home. I should feel triumphant. But it's what they call a Pyrrhic victory. A victory that comes at a very high cost. Our family is broken, and I don't know if we will ever be whole again. I have a hollow feeling that I don't think even the endless horizon on the sea will fill.

The Road Home

THE TRAILER PARK is called Home Place because, the guy who gives us the keys to the trailer says, they want everyone to feel at home here. Since most of the residents had been living in shelters, coming here must feel like heaven. But as soon as we drive up, I understand everything Mama said. This is a place you go when you've got no other choice. My heart kept telling me I didn't have another choice. But now I'm not so sure.

Home Place is just outside Bellvoir, where an old strip mall stood until it got torn down years ago. They placed the trailers on top of the barren pavement, put a chain-link fence around the whole lot, and voilà, a home place. Row after row of trailers, almost as far as the eye can see. There are streets of a certain kind laid out between the trailers, with stop signs and everything. Everyone pulls their car up to their trailer: beat-up old sedans with windows missing, trucks, shiny new cars. Judging by the cars, there are people here who you can tell probably had nice houses and steady jobs before the storm and then there are people here who were poor. Then there are people like us, somewhere in the middle.

Our trailer is toward the back, on Twelfth Street, the guy in the office called it, unit 1218. We drive back there, passing a few people who wave, others who nod or stare at us intently. Older folks, moms with little kids clustered together.

It's hard to identify which trailer is ours. They all look just the same, of course. We walk up the makeshift wooden steps and crack open the door. A smell blasts out at us — that plastic, new car smell. The trailer is long and narrow, but they pack a lot into it. It feels more like a real house than you would think. On one end there's a bedroom with a big double bed and on the other a bedroom with a set of bunk beds. That's my room.

Daddy sits down at the table, runs his hand through his hair, and looks up at me. It's a complicated look — part sad, part resigned, and part relieved. He motions for me to come over. I sit on his lap and rest my head on his chest. "I know I was against your coming," he says. "But I'm glad you're here."

"It's going to be OK, Daddy," I say because there is nothing else to say.

We put our stuff away and it feels like the walls start to close in on me a little. But less than an hour passes before there's a knock at the door. I peek through the window. It's Kendra and Ms. Denise. I yank the door open and fall into Ms. Denise's very firm hug. Then into Kendra. Nothing has changed with them. *This* feels like home.

They start handing in a bunch of bags of stuff they brought over "to make the place more homey," Ms. Denise says: curtains in a cheery red, scented candles, knickknacks, bags and bags of groceries. When they moved into their new place on the base, she says, people gave them so much stuff, they had lots of extras. "So I'm regifting." She laughs with her big hearty laugh. Before I know it, she's gone out to her car, brought in a slow cooker filled with gumbo, and plugged it in.

Kendra and I go back to my "room" to hang out. "So," she says, "here we are."

We exchange a look, a sort of *OK, now what?* look, and burst into laughter, then the moment passes and we're quiet again.

"We're going to pick up where we left off," Kendra says. "Katrina didn't give us a choice. She *made* us leave. Coming back says *you can't beat us.* We're stronger than that."

All those years of being a team player has made her good at pep talks. My mind goes back to that conversation in the hammock in Grandpere's orange grove, a lifetime ago, when we thought this was going to be *our* year. I know we can't really pick up where we left off. We've been damaged. We've changed. But here we are.

When we come back out to the kitchen, Ms. Denise and Daddy are very serious, and I can tell they've been talking about Mama and Mandy. I notice Ms. Denise pats Daddy on the hand. "God has a plan for you," she says. "You'll see."

Then we all eat the best gumbo I've had since we left last summer.

They won't let you down the road to Bayou Perdu without a boat registration — people were coming in to steal washed-up, abandoned boats. After they let us pass, my spirits start to lift. Signs of home. The cows are still on top of the levee. If you squint — if you look past the rubble — you can almost imagine that home is just like it always was. Almost. When we get to the marina, there are still heaps of broken boats up on blocks in the parking lot. But there's a different feeling from the last time we were here. It has that buzz that happens right before shrimping season. People are not just repairing; they're preparing. It feels hopeful. My heart still feels heavy, but I'm a little lighter on my feet.

There's construction going on over where the bait shop

was: they're building a new one. For now it's operating out of a trailer, like everything else. When we walk in, Joe, the guy who owns the shop, comes over and hugs us both. He's been here the whole time, he says, came back before the water drained. A lot of guys are making money on the side repairing and selling salvaged boat parts, he says. Daddy nods, taking it all in. He could do that, I can tell he's thinking. There are so many things he could do here, things he knows how to do. He's in his element. I see a little light creeping back into his eyes. "You need to check out the *Second Wind*," says Joe. "Up on blocks at the end of the parking lot. Might be just the right boat to replace the *Mandy*."

We find her where Joe said she'd be. She looks rough, old, abandoned. Her wheelhouse is in tatters. The rigging is completely destroyed. The hull is miraculously OK, though, and that's what matters. All the rest can be fixed. Yes, we'll take her, Daddy says. There are just a few weeks before brown-shrimp season starts.

But today we are going to get out on the water the only way we can. Sheriff Guidry has been keeping an eye on the pirogue that Katrina spared us from the back of our gutted house. And he even had it fitted with a little outboard motor, so we could use it like a skiff. We retrieve it from the sheriff's department boatshed and push out into the water, slowly, slowly. I close my eyes and feel the wind in my hair. *Inexpressible sweetness*. Like rain on parched ground, color bleeding back into black and white. The pelicans wing above, and there's a flock of tiny plovers diving in unison. They are back for the spring, and so am I.

It is changed, though. The channels are shallower than they used to be. The places where you could have taken a bigger trawler like the *Mandy,* you could probably only take in the *Evangeline* now, if she was still around. The water was so powerful, it picked up ten feet of sediment and dumped it somewhere new. The banks have eroded—the way into the back bayou probably lost forty feet. There was a big marsh that's now an open bay. All the places I used to know have shape-shifted. Katrina bent and broke the people and the land, and we've all had to re-form ourselves.

"Can we find Bayou Valse d'Oiseau?" I ask Daddy.

He seems to have some internal compass. He guides us through the channels until I'm sure we're lost and we'll run out of gas. But then, up ahead, there are islands, and we float into a bay dotted with white. Birds everywhere, hundreds and hundreds of birds. I don't know if it's exactly our bayou. The land looks different. But it doesn't matter. The birds are here. There was enough grass and reeds for them to make their nests. The mama birds are roosting. They're all making a racket—chirping, squawking, chattering, hooting. "They came back," I say.

Daddy smiles. It's the first time I've seen him smile like that since last summer. "They always come back, darlin'. They're always going to come back. I promise."

We fish, catch our supper, and talk, just like the old times.

Then, out of nowhere, he says, "It's happened before that we've been apart for a while." It's as if he's said out loud that last part of a conversation that he'd been having inside his head. "I believe we are going to find some way forward together as a family. That way just hasn't appeared yet."

I nod. I don't really know what to say.

We go quiet again.

"Could we go to Baton Rouge for the weekend sometime? Maybe to look at LSU?" As far as he knows, Mandy will be going there in the fall, and I know he hopes I'll be going there one day, too.

Daddy looks surprised. "Sure," he says hesitantly. "We could do that." Then he gives me a curious look. "I'm thinking that maybe this has something to do with a boy?"

I laugh. "What makes you think that?"

"Darlin', I've been so caught up in my own troubles, I didn't even notice that you had a broken heart. But I see it now."

"It wasn't him," I say quickly. "It wasn't his fault. His family just had to leave and he couldn't let me know."

"It better not be him," Daddy says. Then he puts on his really bad Mafia accent from his favorite movie, *The Godfather*. "Because if he hurts my little girl, he'll be sleepin' with the fishes."

"No, you'd like him, Daddy," I say. "He's a lot like you." I tell him what Tru told me about the Nguyens' fishing and shrimping business up in St. Bernard, how they found a boat they thought they could fix up and get out on the water by white-shrimp season. You could still get in a good season if you did that, I say.

He smiles and shakes his head. "You're so much like me, poor thing. You've just got the water in your blood and shrimp on the brain."

Monday morning, I wait at the bus stop with about twenty other kids from Home Place who are going to Bellvoir Middle and High. I see three people from Bayou Perdu High, including this guy Shane who was on the football team. He comes over and hugs me even though he has never spoken to me in my life.

"Hey, where's your sister?" is the first thing he says. When I tell him, he looks disappointed and drifts away toward the other side of the bus stop.

On the way into school, we pass damaged houses with trailers parked in the front yard — people are living in them until their repairs are done. Every telephone pole has little fliers stapled to it advertising services: demolition or debris removal, boat salvage. But I see that people are living out of all kinds of other vehicles, too: abandoned school buses, vans. There are heaps of garbage and rubble everywhere. Steps leading nowhere, everywhere. Everything that used to be in a building seems to be in a trailer now: the church, the town offices, clinics. Everything is temporary.

Bellvoir High is like a middle ground between Bayou Perdu and Brookdale. It's nicer and newer than Bayou Perdu, but nowhere near as fancy as Brookdale. It's bigger than Bayou Perdu, but not as big as Brookdale. The kids are a lot richer than at Bayou Perdu—you can tell by the cars in the parking lot—but not as rich as at Brookdale. I can pretty much guarantee they don't have yoga for PE here.

While the secretary at Brookdale seemed to go out of her way to point out my Katrina refugee status, the one here could care less. She probably gets new students dribbling in every day. "Address?" she asks without looking up.

It occurs to me that I don't know it.

"You at Home Place?" she asks.

I nod.

"What unit?"

I tell her and she scrawls something on my papers and shoves them back across the counter to me.

I see familiar faces in a lot of my classes. Some of them light up when they see me; people come up and say hi or hug me. I find Kendra in the hall and we hug and tease each other about our new uniforms. *I'm back. I did the right thing.* But deep inside, I have doubts.

At lunch, Kendra introduces me to her basketball friends, several of them her former rivals.

"You don't play, do you?" a girl called Delia says.

I shake my head. She turns to the girls next to her and starts talking. Apparently our conversation is over. All day I feel like I'm trailing Kendra, a puppy dog at her heels. She has this built-in group with basketball. I just have her.

The bus drops us back at Home Place after school, and everyone shuffles off down their different rows to their trailers. I can hear fighting coming from inside some of the trailers I pass on the way back from the bus stop, when someone opens a door or a window. Even when they're closed. Someone is cursing over some small inconvenience: "Why'd you let the damn cat out?" or "Can't you even make toast without burning it?" But when I get back inside our trailer, it's quiet. So lonely. I try texting Danielle a few times to let her know I got back. But there's no response. She's in a different time zone. Still in school, I guess. Kendra is already working again, so I feel like I'll never see her in the afternoons.

When I'm done with my homework, I go outside to look around. There are a few little kids circling on bikes at the big empty pavement where the rows of trailers end. A few little boys chasing lizards. I start to walk aimlessly. The sun is beating down on me. There's no shade here; the only trees are beyond the fence. I walk over, touch that chalky metal wire, shake the chain links, and have the sudden urge to climb over it, to get to those trees beyond, even if they're just scraggly little scrubby ones. I try to hoist myself up, but there's nowhere to get a foothold. I cross the scorching-hot pavement, starting to sweat, and exit out the front gate, past the heaps of trash and dead branches on the side of the road, all the way around the back of the fence. I sit under the not-very-shady trees. There are flies and mosquitos buzzing all around me, and I can barely stand it for a second. After all that work to get here.

I walk back around that ugly fence, into the ugly trailer park that's now my home, and I feel so lost, so utterly lost. The pavement stretches out for what seems like miles in front of me, and I am looking at my feet, putting one in front of the other. Then something catches my eye. Coming up through a crack in that endless stretch of hot concrete is a single, delicate pink flower. I stoop and take a closer look. Somehow, the seed of it shimmied down into that crack and took root. Somehow it sought the light and pushed its way up and blossomed. It is all alone out here in this big, barren place, but it is blooming.

Daddy doesn't get home till late and I have to admit, it's kind of scary here. The lady two trailers down, Ms. Burns, told me she sleeps with knives under her mattress. She put a welcome mat and potted plants outside her trailer and someone stole them. There's a security officer who rides up and down the "streets" on a golf cart at night. But I don't feel safe. It's because we don't really know each other. People don't really trust each other, either. I guess when you've been through what some of them have been through, it would be hard to trust.

The next day at school, I wonder if I should talk to the counselor here. Maybe she's like Ms. Bell. But when I go into her office, I know that I won't. She's this blank-faced woman who says, "Can I help you?" in a way that makes it clear that's the last thing she wants to do. "Just wondering about signing up for the SAT," I say, and she hands me a brochure. Feeling a little desperate that afternoon alone in the trailer, I call Ms. Bell. "It's Evangeline Riley," I say.

"Evangeline! I'm so glad you called. I've been wondering about you. How's it going down there?"

I tell her about school, the trailer park. How things aren't how I thought they'd be, and how the counselor at Bellvoir isn't like her.

"Not every counselor is the right one for every person," she says. "Maybe you could try something else. Doing something you enjoy, that makes you happy. Fixing up the boat. Physical exercise and connection to things you enjoy can be really therapeutic."

She always seems to know the right thing to say.

I put an ad up on the bulletin board at school. RIDE NEEDED TO MARINA AFTER SCHOOL. WILL PAY FOR GAS. I wait a few days, but no one gets in touch. Then I hear the cafeteria ladies talking while I'm in line for lunch one day, and one of them is saying how she's helping her husband rebuild their boat. "Do you go down there in the afternoons?" I blurt out. She looks annoyed, but she says she does. So after some negotiations, I am riding to the marina with Ms. Dolores, who makes me call her that rather than Dolores. She's grumpy and hardly speaks the whole time.

When I show up at the marina for the first time, Daddy shakes his head. "I'm here to work," I say.

He looks at the ground, then back up at me. "Well, we've got plenty of that to do around here."

I learn to sand fiberglass. I scrounge around for parts and help Daddy put them in. I mend the damaged nets we bought secondhand to save money. Sometimes we fish. I am exhausted at the end of the day. But I feel more alive than I have in months. I'm learning a new way to live in the place I'll always call home.

So there are signs of hope, like that little flower. There are a few charters going out again at the marina — can't keep the sports fishermen away when it's their season. It's in their nature to get back out on the water. Like it's in mine.

One day, Daddy goes up to Algiers for a part and I go out on the water and get that sense of peace and clarity I always find on the water. But I can't sleep that night. No dogs are allowed in the trailer park, but they're here anyway. I can hear one howling and howling. I'm restless. I have strange dreams. I can feel the weight and warmth and softness of a body next to me. Surprising, but comforting. It's Mamere, I think sleepily. She kisses me on the forehead and I wake up, confused about where I am. I could swear she was *just* right next to me.

I get up and walk out to Daddy, who I can hear talking

on the phone in the kitchen. I am suddenly afraid. I can't hear what he's saying, but I can hear heaviness in his voice.

"Do you want me to come up there?"

It must be Mama. Something must have happened.

"We'll meet you there. I can start making the arrangements."

It's dark in the kitchen. I can see his outline against the light filtering in from those floodlights near the back fence. I can't see the expression on his face.

"What is it? What happened?" But somehow, before the words come out of his mouth, I know what he is going to say. Mamere is dead. That really was her in my dream. She came to say good-bye.

He grabs my hand. "You better sit down, darlin'."

"Just tell me. Mamere's dead, isn't she?"

He nods. Something inside me shatters.

"No. No." I am shaking my head.

He grabs me, hugs me tight. He's trembling; he's crying. "I'm so sorry, baby."

"That can't be right. What did Mama say?"

"She wasn't feeling well after dinner, and she went upstairs to lie down. When Cel went up to check on her, she was gone. She went off in her sleep. She'd had this heart thing for a while, and she didn't tell anybody about it. Didn't want to worry us."

I start to pace. "But . . . but . . ." She can't be dead. I didn't get to say good-bye.

247

"I'm so sorry, darlin'," Daddy repeats. "You know you meant the world to her."

I sit down on the couch, pull my feet up under me, make myself into a ball. I am rocking back and forth. "What do we do now?"

"They're going to bring her to St. Martinville. We're going to meet them up there. Go back to bed, darlin'. There's nothing we can do now."

But how could I possibly sleep? I can't close my eyes or I'll see her. I stare into space until I go in to wake Daddy up and find that he's awake, too. We throw a few things in bags and head out while it's still dark.

I feel like I'm going to be sick, so I have to close my eyes. The *clop-clop* of the tires over the bridge turns into a soothing rhythm and I drift off. When I wake up, we're somewhere that looks like the suburbs of Baton Rouge. I'm not sure if we're coming up to it or we've already passed it. For a minute, I'm not sure if I dreamed it all. I look at Daddy, his eyes focused on the road.

"Is it true? Is Mamere dead?"

He takes one hand off the wheel and reaches over to touch my shoulder. "Yeah, darlin'. It's true."

I look back out the window, feeling my heart go hard. Maybe it's my punishment. For being so stubborn. For not staying with my mother. For leaving Mamere. I will never forgive myself for this.

We pull up outside Tante Sadie's little brick house in

St. Martinville. She opens the door in her robe—a quilted satiny pink one. Her long silver hair is in braids, the way Mamere used to have them. Her face is somber, but she hasn't been crying. She hugs Daddy wordlessly and strokes my face. "You were her favorite, you know. Her namesake."

She makes coffee as we sit at her tiny kitchen table with a pack of powdered doughnuts open in front of us. "Kenny and the kids are coming in this afternoon," she says. "Fifi's goin' to have the gathering after the funeral at her house."

Funeral. The word stings me. I brace myself for what will be a horrible few days. Then after that, who knows? When I try to look into the future now, I don't see anything.

I go to the funeral home with Daddy to meet with the director. "I'm sorry for your loss," he says as he presses his cold hand into mine. He speaks in a hushed tone, showing us the different options for caskets. Daddy doesn't hesitate, knows what to do. Mamere already has her burial plot, next to Grandpere and near her whole family at St. Martin's. They will take care of everything, the funeral director says— receive the body when it arrives, make sure that the family doesn't have anything more to worry about in our time of grief. I don't say a word the whole time. I feel like I am watching this scene from above. He called Mamere a "body."

We go back to Tante Sadie's house to wait for Mama and Mandy. Whereas I couldn't sleep at all before, now I'm so tired, I can barely move. I lie down in the little pink room upstairs that was Cousin Candy's when she was little. It is perfectly quiet here, perfectly restful. I close my eyes.

When I wake up, I have that disoriented feeling you get when you've slept too long and at the wrong time. I don't know where I am at first. I can hear voices downstairs. It takes me a minute to realize that Mama is here. I walk down the stairs still in a fog and can see her and Daddy on the couch. She is crumpled up next to him, with her head on his chest. She looks like a little girl. He is running his hand through her hair. His eyes are closed. The step creaks under me and they both look up. When Mama's eyes catch mine, I know that the wall between us has washed away. I cross over to her, put my arms around her. She is soft again, the Mama I remember from when I was little, who would tuck me in, who made me my favorite fries at the diner when I was having a tough day. The three of us sit there on the couch together silently, until Mandy comes in with Aunt Sadie with groceries and we snap into doing what needs to be done.

The visitation is at the funeral home the next night. When we pull up, we can hardly find a parking space, there are so many cars. There are people I've never seen before going in, men in suits, people all dressed up. "That's Grandpere's nephew Dell," says Mama. "And his kids. I think that's Delphine, Mamere's cousin. She must be ninety by now." It hits me that I had thought of Mamere as just mine. But her reach was so much further than I ever thought.

My cousin Ami is there greeting people when we walk

in, telling people where to go. She hands me a prayer card, with a Madonna-and-child picture on the front and a picture of Mamere on the back. *In loving memory of Evangeline Arceneaux Beauchamp, devoted wife, mother, sister, grandmother, and teacher.* There's a Bible verse, too:

> *There is a season for everything,*
>   *a time for every occupation under heaven:*
> *A time for giving birth, a time for dying; a time for*
>   *planting, a time for uprooting what has been planted.*
> *A time for killing, a time for healing; a time for knocking*
>   *down, a time for building.*
> *A time for tears, a time for laughter; a time for mourning,*
>   *a time for dancing.*
> *A time for throwing stones away, a time for gathering*
>   *them; a time for embracing, a time to refrain from*
>   *embracing.*
> *A time for searching, a time for losing; a time for keeping,*
>   *a time for discarding.*
> *A time for tearing, a time for sewing; a time for keeping*
>   *silent, a time for speaking.*
> *A time for loving, a time for hating; a time for war, a time*
>   *for peace.*
>
>   —Ecclesiastes 3:1–8

She said that she would come back home when it was time. So that's what she meant. It was her time.

I walk into the gathering room and see the open casket. I have to do this. I have to say good-bye, whether I'm ready or not. It feels like I am the only person in this crowded room as I approach, and I see her there, her hair up in a bun like it always was. She's wearing her Sunday best, a floral dress with a dark jacket over it, her pearl necklace and little pearl earrings. But it strikes me immediately; I don't have any doubt: this isn't Mamere. It may be her body, but it isn't her. What I knew was her spirit, and it isn't contained in this body. It's somewhere else now — it's in me, it's in all these people around me.

I lower myself to the padded kneeler in front of me and make the sign of the cross. *Mamere,* I say inside my head, *I know you can hear me somewhere. I'm sorry I didn't get to say good-bye. I'm sorry I wasn't with you. But I know you're going to be with me always, just in a different way. This isn't really good-bye for us. If I ever need you, I know you're going to be there for me.*

I walk out into the lobby, where Aunt Cel and Uncle Jim, Mama and Daddy are in a receiving line. Someone — probably Aunt Cel — created a poster-board collage of pictures of Mamere throughout her life, and it's leaning on an easel in the lobby. I pore over all the photographs. The big wedding picture of her and Grandpere. Her holding Aunt Cel when she was a baby, her lips dark with lipstick in that black-and-white photo. There's a bunch of her class pictures when she was a teacher, standing on the edge of rows and rows of little kids. Someone taps me on the shoulder. It's Mr. Ray from the gas station in Bayou Perdu. I haven't seen him since the day we were evacuating.

"Hey, darlin'," he says. He has tears in his eyes. "Your grandma was a good woman. She taught me how to read, you know. My mama and daddy didn't know how to read — they couldn't teach me. People looked down on us, 'cause we didn't have nuthin'. But she never did. When I heard she passed, I got in my car and came here. I said that I got to pay my respects to Ms. Beauchamp."

The tears start to well up in my eyes and I have to push them back. Mr. Ray tells me he is living in Baton Rouge now and that he heard about Mamere's passing from Mr. Sumps. Somehow the word has gotten around to people from Bayou Perdu, no matter where they are. What Mr. Ray said is only the first story like that I hear. Miss Helen from the Dollar Store is here. When she was little, she says, Mamere used to give her boxes of Mama and Aunt Cel's old clothes because she only had one thing to wear and it smelled bad and the other kids made fun of her. This woman I'd never met tells me that Mamere would bring her the leftovers from the diner so she could feed her kids. She's sobbing the whole time she tells the story. The retired superintendent of schools from the parish is here. He tells me that when they rebuild the elementary school — and they will rebuild, he says — he's going to recommend that they name it after Mamere. In those hours, I learn that my sweet little old Cajun grandma was the one who was secretly a superhero.

The funeral is packed, so many people that some are standing at the back of the big old church. Grandpere's remaining brothers—there were six of them, now three, my great-uncles—my great-aunts, their children and their children's children, cousins, former students, people from Bayou Perdu. Mrs. Menil comes wobbling down the aisle, supported by Delbert, and plops herself across from us. Delbert smiles sympathetically at me. I smile back.

Mandy sits next to me and holds my hand. Daddy and Mama are on the other side of her. They are holding hands, too. Daddy reaches for Mandy, and together we form an unbroken chain. We sing all Mamere's favorite hymns—"Amazing Grace" and "Make Me a Channel of Your Peace." There are three priests, so old they can barely stand up. We follow the casket out to the cemetery behind the church, passing all those dead Evangelines. She and Grandpere share a headstone. Her name was already right there next to his. They only had to fill in the year. She came back to St. Martinville, just like she said she would. When it was her time.

When it's over, we go back to Tante Fifi's house. The cars line the side of the street. The doors are open and people come and go. The dining room table is practically groaning from the weight of the food everybody has brought:

there's gumbo, jambalaya, boudin, tasso, red beans and rice, chicken. Nobody is going to go hungry. Mama and Daddy are talking to cousins. Mandy and I go sit on the front steps together.

"So did you tell Mama? About LSU?" I say.

She nods.

"How'd that go?"

"Not great," she says. She looks off into the distance. "But I do have a plan. There's this school in Atlanta. It's not too late to apply to it, and Aunt Cel said I could live at her house in the fall for free if I wanted to go there while I apply for LSU again. People drop out freshman year, so there are spaces. If you get good grades."

"Why would you live with her, though? Wouldn't you and Mama stay at the town house?"

"I don't know. . . ." She looks around, making sure that Mama and Daddy aren't within earshot. "Mama hasn't been happy since you left. She's thinking of coming back. I heard her on the phone one night when she didn't know I was listening. Apparently someone at the chicken company knows someone who does the catering at one of those golf courses in New Orleans, and they need someone to manage the dining room. She's talking about doing it. The pay is pretty good."

My heart skips a beat. "She said that?"

Mandy nods.

"Would you want to stay in Atlanta with Aunt Cel?"

She stares out into the yard. "Chris is going to Auburn

next year, which is only two hours away. But if I came back to Louisiana, it would be like five hours away."

I want to tell her not to plan her life around this guy. But I stop myself. Mandy needs to do things her way, just like I need to do them mine. I smile and put my arm around her shoulder.

From the back of the house, I hear the strains of an accordion. We follow the music out the back door onto the patio. It's an older guy playing; I think he is one of Grandpere's nephews. He plays something slow, a little mournful, but so soothing. One of Mama's cousins — Tante Marie's son Joseph — comes down with a fiddle and joins. Mamere would have loved this. Like when we were little and Grandpere and his friends used to play on the porch. When they take a break, I approach Joseph.

"Did you ever know this song that Grandpere wrote for Mamere?" I ask. "Called the 'Sweet Evangeline Waltz'?"

He smiles. "My daddy used to play that with Uncle Claude," he says.

He and the other cousin, whose name is Russ, start playing it. It's a few minutes later when I see some of the old folks get up to dance. They are spinning slowly around, looking into each other's eyes or holding on to each other. Then I notice out of the corner of my eye that Mama and Daddy have gotten up to dance. It's like they don't see anyone around them, they're in their own little world, looking at each other, completely absorbed. They love each other. They still do.

I start to drift toward the hammock in the back of Tante Fifi's yard, to be alone, away from everyone. The music follows me, haunting me, a ghost of Grandpere and Mamere. A friendly ghost. In the hammock, I lie down and look up through the trees. I rock a little, pushing off from the ground with my foot. I close my eyes, feel the breeze on my face, hear the music in the distance. The warmth surrounds me. I feel completely blank. Then the buzzing of my phone near my hip breaks the silence.

"Hey." It's Tru.

"Hi." I am stepping into a moment that I knew was waiting for me.

"It's Tru."

"I know."

"Is this a good time? You sound . . . I don't know. Where are you?"

I sit up. "I'm in St. Martinville." I know I sound flat, not like I should sound when I am hearing his voice for the first time in months. "Mamere died. The funeral just ended." It comes out with a crack, a creak in my voice.

"What? Oh, my God." There is panic in his voice. "I'm so sorry. I . . . Can I come see you?"

Ms. Bell's words come back to me: *It's OK to ask for help.* "Please come. Come now."

"I'll be there in an hour and a half."

"OK," I say, surrendering to whatever comes next.

"Wait, where should I meet you?"

And there's only one thing that pops into my mind. The Evangeline Oak.

"I'm going for a walk to get a little fresh air," I whisper to Mandy in the kitchen. "If anyone asks, I'll be back soon."

I leave the house with nothing, not even my purse, walking down the sidewalk toward town with the shadows growing long. The houses on Tante Fifi's street are big and pretty and settled, with tall trees in the yards, and grass. The azaleas are in bloom.

I reach the sleepy little downtown. There are a few restaurants, shops open. Some people are sitting outside because it's nice out. I catch a glimpse of myself in the window of the floral shop. I forgot that I was still in my funeral clothes. I look older than myself. I feel older. Older than I did yesterday.

At the side of the church, I stop at the Evangeline statue. There she is, in her cloak and her wooden shoes, staring off with her blank stone eyes. She sits atop what's supposed to be the tomb of Emmeline Labiche, whom Longfellow based his poem on, but everyone says that the tomb is empty. I look back into the graveyard. There is the canopy over Mamere's grave. I have to look away.

The heels I wore to the funeral are starting to hurt, so I take off my shoes and walk barefoot toward Evangeline Oak

Park. The light has gone that soft, late-afternoon orange. There's a walkway up to the tree, so massive and ancient-looking, its broad branches stretching out, ivy crawling up its trunk. I was here many times as a kid, when we visited St. Martinville with Mamere and Grandpere. "Not every girl has a tree named after her," Grandpere said. "You and your *mamere,* you're special." It did make me feel special to see my name on the sign:

EVANGELINE OAK — LONGFELLOW'S POEM "EVANGELINE"
IMMORTALIZED THE TRAGEDY OF THE ACADIAN EXILE
FROM NOVA SCOTIA IN 1755. THIS OAK MARKS THE LEGENDARY
MEETING PLACE OF EMMELINE LABICHE AND LOUIS ARCENEAUX,
THE COUNTERPARTS OF EVANGELINE AND GABRIEL.

There's a gazebo across from the tree and a bust of Longfellow nearby.

I wander for a few minutes, go look at the Bayou Teche, the river that brought my ancestors, depositing them here from Canada, the way the Mississippi brought all those little bits of Iowa and Missouri down and deposited them in Bayou Perdu. All those currents flowing, never stopping. I imagine seeing those rivers from above, the way a bird does, seeing the way they connect and flow together and empty into the ocean. But from here, it's so hard to see anything more than what's right in front of you.

I hear a car door shut in the parking lot and start back

toward the tree. I see him coming down the path. He's wearing jeans and a white T-shirt. His hair has gotten longer. He waves and I start to move toward him, not really running, but not slow. His pace quickens, too, and then we are together, like two puzzle pieces finally fitting seamlessly.

His arms are around me, lean and strong, and I bury my face in his chest.

That storm, that big, swirling cloud, is inside me. As I hold on to him, it rips through me. It tears down every wall I've built up in this last horrible year and I fall to pieces, sobbing. Every disappointment, every dashed hope, every failure, every loss is flooding out of me. It overtakes me. I couldn't stop it if I tried. But I don't try. I let go. I let it out. I hold on to him. He holds on to me, and strokes my hair. He doesn't say anything. We sit on the steps and I keep crying, and he keeps holding on to me. It keeps coming and coming, and then it eases up. It slows to a trickle and I can breathe again.

A strange feeling comes over me — emptiness, but not a sad one. An emptiness that is newness, that's ready to be filled up with something else now that all that pain has come out. I look up at Tru. My face is puffy, probably hideous. I've never felt so naked. And he kisses me, softly, the kiss that I imagined so many times, much stronger than I ever imagined it. We still haven't said a word to each other. But we look into each other's eyes, his eyes so warm, so real. I feel like we don't have to. "I know," he says finally. "I know."

We walk down to the river, arm in arm, still not saying a word, but it doesn't feel awkward. It's like we have to
let the physical presence of each other settle in for a while.
My shoulder fits perfectly under his arm. We walk at exactly
the same pace, completely in sync, and we stop and look out
over the river.

"So much happened when we left Atlanta. You know, I
tried to reach you. I sent you a bunch of e-mails."

"I just got them. I wrote you back."

"My e-mail was disconnected when I left school. I'm not
in school. I've been working, washing dishes and driving a
forklift, so I could help make money for a new boat."

"Then how did you . . . ?"

"My dad was talking to his cousin, Hip's mom, last night.
Hip got on and asked to talk to me. He said you called. He
gave me your number."

"That was back in December. He told me Kaye Pham
was in Baton Rouge. I called her to ask if she'd seen you. . . ."

"I see her every week at church. She never told me you
called her."

"Her friend Elly told me that you two were together and
I should stop trying to contact you."

"What?" He looks furious. "I've barely even had a conversation with her. Did you believe her?"

"For a while. I thought you had just left and moved on.
Until I got your e-mails."

"Never," he says. "I never stopped thinking about you.

I never wanted to be with anyone else." He shakes his head.

We look at each other with this sort of sad, disbelieving look. A big, destructive swirling cloud tore our families apart and brought us together. I believe right now that we both believe that nothing can keep us apart. We belong together.

He looks away for a moment. "I wish I could stay. I don't want to leave. At all. I have to work tonight though. But I would drive all night to see you again."

"That sounds like a line from a song."

We kiss again. "Hang on," he says. "Stay right there. I'll be right back."

I watch him run off to the parking lot, feeling the peace of the wings of a big white bird folding over me. He comes back a few minutes later, his guitar strapped over his shoulder. I can feel my face stretching into a smile.

We sit down by the river, and I dip my sore feet in the cold water. The sky is bruised purple and blue now as the light fades.

"Remember I had that song that I was going to play for you that night?"

"When I didn't show up?"

"No, it's OK. Besides, I think that happened for a reason. So I wouldn't play you that awful song."

"It couldn't have been awful if you wrote it."

"No, it was. It's that thing that I told you. I was imitating the style and the lyrics, all the music I knew from Mr.

Monks and from my mom's records. It didn't sound quite right because it wasn't from me."

He pulls his guitar into his lap and he's looking down at the strings. "Everything that's happened since the storm . . . it's like the greatest material for a blues song. Losing the house, the whole town, moving, again and again. Everything. Being apart from you." He holds me in his gaze, so serious. "There were some nights when I thought I couldn't go on anymore. I'd pick up the guitar and play and try to write songs. You'd think that the blues would fit me more than they ever have, but what came out was different."

He strums a little and that look comes over him, like I saw that night at Chase's house, like he doesn't notice anyone else around him. He's consumed in his thoughts. "So I wrote this new one for you."

It is soft, gentle, like a boat rocking on water, over the waves, with a sureness, a rightness. It is that beautiful sadness that pierces your heart but makes it soar at the same time. It's about a sailor who's lost at sea. He's drifting, and all he can think about is the girl who will be waiting when he finally gets back to shore. Because he's decided that she's his home now. Every chord rings with this fierce, fierce love. The kind of love that would hold you up your whole life no matter what came along.

It's called "The Ballad of Evangeline."

Two Years Later

I'VE NEVER FORGOTTEN that conversation about fate I had with Tru when we were in Atlanta — that maybe fate was catching up to the things you love. I'm one of the six thousand freshmen at LSU this fall. Tru is one of the others. And we are together.

I have a collection of heavy and expensive books about marine biology and ornithology. I've got the Mississippi River flowing close to me again; close enough that when I walk out of my dorm, I can feel the breeze off of it, walk to the levee, watch the barges go by and scan the sky for birds heading down the flyway. And I've got plans. Big plans. Next summer, I'll be an intern for one of my professors, working on a project looking at how coastal erosion is affecting migratory birds.

I still see Kendra, who's at Southern on her amazing basketball scholarship, although not as much as I'd like to. I can feel life pulling us apart, but she will still show up at my door and come in without knocking, throw herself down on my bed, and say, "I'm hungry. Anything to eat around here?" So far we have gone home two weekends together, once for Bellvoir homecoming and once just because. Our next trip to New Orleans is scheduled for November, when the Derek Turner Project will be playing at the Royal Sonesta in the Quarter. Guess who's playing piano with him?

Mandy will be back from Atlanta next month for the Orange Queen competition. She thinks she's really got a chance this year.

Every once in a while I'll get a call or a text from Danielle. She's going to a community college in Salt Lake City while she tries to decide what she wants to major in. She sends me pictures of her cute little sister, whom she adores and who clearly adores her, too. I am so glad she has a *real* sister to love her like that. I know that we are not going to get back what we once had. I know we may never be in the same place again. But I also know that for each of us, the other is part of what we'll always call home.

Our family's home now is a duplex on the outskirts of Bellvoir. It went up at the end of last year, brand new, granite countertops and all. It takes Mama less time to get to work in New Orleans than it did in Atlanta. Daddy can be at the marina in about an hour and when I visit home, I'm always there helping him, getting out on the water or fixing up boats, which I've now become pretty good at. Shrimping is the same as it's always been, up and down, scraping by. But it's in him. I can't say that Mama and Daddy are who they used to be. But they are trying. Maybe that's all anybody can do.

Ground has been broken on Evangeline Beauchamp Elementary near Bayou Perdu. Not enough kids have come back to make a whole new school, so all the kids from the south part of the parish will go to this one. When they do the ribbon cutting, the superintendent says that we can plant an orange tree out front. Mamere would have liked that.

Sometimes I take out the copy of *Evangeline* she gave me on my sixteenth birthday and leaf through it. It can't replace her warmth or the comfort she always gave me, but it feels like a part of her that I can still hold in my hands. When she gave it to me, she didn't know that it would be one of the only material things I'd be able to keep from my old life. I always thought she wanted me to have it so that I'd be proud of my heritage and my name—the girl in a book. But now I think it was to remind me that loss and longing are a part of everyone's story. And that no matter how broken

I might feel, I can still find the inexpressible sweetness that the first Evangeline found, even when things seemed the darkest. Maybe it will come like it did for her, in a moment when the setting sun turns the sky and the water golden and a birdsong pierces through the silence right into my heart. Or maybe it will come with a kiss after an impossible-to-bear separation. But in all the low times, and the in-between times, those moments will echo through me like a melody.

ACKNOWLEDGMENTS

I wish I could be like Tru and write a song of love and gratitude to all those who helped me all the way through my first thoughts of trying to write fiction to finishing this book. It would be a lengthy ballad, with high and low notes and occasional dissonance, ultimately with a happy ending. But I'm no songwriter, so I'm just going to have to break this down into parts.

The chorus of this song I'd write is full of supporters who were encouraging from the earliest drafts, especially my writing group: Bethany Dellinger, Susan Stewart, Susan Lefler, Art Grand, and Karen Miller, to whom I'm extra grateful for reading multiple drafts and for providing insightful comments without which I couldn't have gone forward. My brilliant cousin, Sue Corbett, had the thankless job of reading awful first drafts of multiple efforts and gave me some of the best advice; I am grateful for her encouragement, her time, and for inspiring me to try to do this in the first place. Thanks, too, go to Anne Slatton for reading a draft and teaching me everything I know about writing dialogue and to Dawn Cusick for being my sounding board.

My agent, Claire Anderson-Wheeler, saw potential in a not-quite-ready story and with incredibly sharp vision helped me shape it into something that works. Her support and belief in me means everything. I am the luckiest author I know.

Thank you to my brilliant editor, Katie Cunningham, for her insight and understanding of the story I was trying to tell and for making it better. Thank you for believing in this book and bringing it into the world. And thank you to Hannah Mahoney and Maggie Deslaurier for their keen eyes, Sherry Fatla for the interior design, Matt Roeser for the cover, and the whole crew at Candlewick.

Thank you to my family and friends.

Finally, to Andrew for always supporting and believing in me and never asking to read it. And to Maeve and Finn for inspiring me to stick with it. This little family is the sweet melody in my life that makes my heart sing.